D1421274

Wildfire Island Docs

Welcome to Paradise!

Meet the small but dedicated team of medics who service the remote Pacific Wildfire Island.

In this idyllic setting relationships are rekindled, passions are stirred, and bonds that will last a lifetime are forged in the tropical heat…

But there's also a darker side to paradise—secrets, lies and greed amidst the Lockhart family threaten the community, and the team find themselves fighting to save more than the lives of their patients. They must band together to fight for the future of the island they've all come to call home!

Read Caroline and Keanu's story in
The Man She Could Never Forget
by Meredith Webber

Read Anna and Luke's story in
The Nurse Who Stole His Heart
by Alison Roberts

And watch for more
fabulous *Wildfire Island Docs* stories
coming soon from Mills & Boon Medical Romance!

Dear Reader,

In March 2014, a group of writers from far-flung parts of the country were meeting up for their eighth or ninth writers' retreat…The first retreat originated when four of us got together for the Crocodile Creek series of books, and with other friends invited it became a yearly event—a week somewhere near a beach, for brainstorming, writing, an occasional sip of wine and, recently, great lobster for lunch at a nearby restaurant.

So there we were, Marion Lennox, Alison Roberts and myself, amongst our other friends, with a vague idea of doing something together again—a series…six books…a tropical island. We threw some ideas around, wrote notes, drew island pictures and then went home—thousands of kilometres from each other but still in touch. About halfway through that year we got serious enough to actually work out a few overall continuity ideas, and each of us decided on our characters and the bare bones of a plot for our own story.

I think it was Marion who put it all together and sent if off for editorial approval—which we got, with a few stipulations. Then began the fun of fitting the books in with already scheduled books and getting the stories written. My workload at the time was lightest, so I said I would do the first book—setting up the island itself, introducing the characters who would be in most of the books and generally getting started.

So here, lucky reader, is the first of six books set on Wildfire Island, a small island in the M'Langi group, way out in the Pacific Ocean. Privately owned, the island is falling on hard times and in need of rescue—so rescuing it and rescues of another kind are a thread running through the books.

Enjoy!

Meredith Webber

THE MAN
SHE COULD
NEVER FORGET

BY
MEREDITH WEBBER

All rights reserved including the right of reproduction in whole
or in part in any form. This edition is published by arrangement with
Harlequin Books S.A.

This is a work of fiction. Names, characters, places, locations and
incidents are purely fictional and bear no relationship to any real
life individuals, living or dead, or to any actual places, business
establishments, locations, events or incidents. Any resemblance is
entirely coincidental.

This book is sold subject to the condition that it shall not, by way of
trade or otherwise, be lent, resold, hired out or otherwise circulated
without the prior consent of the publisher in any form of binding or
cover other than that in which it is published and without a similar
condition including this condition being imposed on the subsequent
purchaser.

® and TM are trademarks owned and used by the trademark owner
and/or its licensee. Trademarks marked with ® are registered with the
United Kingdom Patent Office and/or the Office for Harmonisation in
the Internal Market and in other countries.

First published in Great Britain 2016
By Mills & Boon, an imprint of HarperCollins*Publishers*
1 London Bridge Street, London, SE1 9GF

© 2016 Meredith Webber

ISBN: 978-0-263-26366-4

Our policy is to use papers that are natural, renewable and recyclable
products and made from wood grown in sustainable forests. The logging
and manufacturing processes conform to the legal environmental
regulations of the country of origin.

Printed and bound in Great Britain
by CPI Antony Rowe, Chippenham, Wiltshire

Meredith Webber lives on the sunny Gold Coast in Queensland, Australia, but takes regular trips west into the Outback, fossicking for gold or opals. These breaks in the beautiful and sometimes cruel red earth country provide an escape from the writing desk and a chance for the mind to roam free—not to mention getting some much needed exercise. They also supply the kernels of so many stories she finds it's hard to stop writing!

Books by Meredith Webber

Mills & Boon Medical Romance

Taming Dr Tempest
Melting the Argentine Doctor's Heart
Orphan Under the Christmas Tree
New Doc in Town
The Sheikh and the Surrogate Mum
Christmas Where She Belongs
One Baby Step at a Time
Date with a Surgeon Prince
The Accidental Daddy
The Sheikh Doctor's Bride
The One Man to Heal Her

Visit the Author Profile page
at millsandboon.co.uk for more titles.

DUNDEE CITY COUNCIL

LEISURE READING

ACCESSION NUMBER

C00 948784X

SUPPLIER: Magna
PRICE: 64.50
CLASS No. 823.91
DATE 20/1/16

To Linda and Alison and the writing friends
we share and love—long may Maytone survive!

**Praise for
Meredith Webber**

'The romance is emotional, passionate, and does not
appear to be forced as everything happens gradually
and naturally. The author's fans and everyone who
loves sheikh romance are gonna love this one.'
—*HarlequinJunkie* on
The Sheikh Doctor's Bride

'*The One Man to Heal Her* by Meredith Webber was a
well-written romance with a well-constructed storyline
which was both enjoyable and believable.'
—*HarlequinJunkie*

CHAPTER ONE

As THE SMALL plane circled above the island, the hard lumps of pain and worry that had been lodged in Caroline Lockhart's chest for the past months dissolved in the delight of seeing her home.

From the air, the island looked like a precious jewel set in an emerald-green sea. The white coral sand of the beaches at the northern end gleamed like a ribbon tying a very special parcel, the lush tropical forest providing the green wrapping paper.

Coming in from the west, they passed over the red cliffs that lit up so brilliantly at sunset that early sailors had called the island Wildfire.

As they flew closer, she could pick out the buildings.

The easiest to find was the palatial Lockhart mansion, built by her great-grandfather on a plateau on the southern tip of the island after he'd bought it from the M'Langi people who had found it too rough to settle.

Lockhart House—her home for so many years—the only real home she'd known as a child.

The house sat at the very highest point on the plateau, with views out over the sea, ocean waves breaking against the encircling reef, and beyond them the dots of other islands, big and small, settled and uninhabited, that, with Wildfire, made up the M'Langi group.

Immediately below the house and almost hidden by the thick rainforest surrounding it was the lagoon—its colour dependent on the sky above, so today it was a deep, dark blue.

Grandma's lagoon.

In truth it was a crater lake from the days of volcanic action in the area, but Grandma had loved her lagoon and had refused to call it anything else.

Below the house and lagoon was the hospital her father, Max Lockhart, had given his life to building, a memorial to his dead wife—Caroline's mother.

Around the main hospital building its cluster of staff villas crowded like chickens around a mother hen. And below that again lay the airstrip.

Farther north, where the plateau flattened as it reached the sea, sat the research station with the big laboratory building, the kitchen and recreation hut, small cabins dotted along the beach to accommodate visiting scientists.

The research station catered to any scientists interested in studying health issues unique to this group of isolated islands, and the tropical diseases prevalent here.

The most intensive research had been on the effects of M'Langi tea—made from the bark of a particular tree—and why the islanders who drank this concoction regularly seemed to be less affected by the mosquitos, which carried a unique strain of encephalitis.

As she frowned at what appeared to be changes to the research station, she wondered if anyone was still working there. Keanu's father had been the first to show interest in the tea—

Keanu.

She shook her head as if to dislodge memories of Keanu from her head and tried to think who might be there now. According to her father, a man she knew only as Luke had been working there for a short time but that had been four or five years ago.

Circling back to the southern end of the island, past the little village that had grown up after Opuru Island had been evacuated after a tsunami, she could just pick out the entrance to the gold mine that tunnelled deep beneath the plateau.

The mine had brought wealth not only to her family but to the islanders as well, but the only sign of it was a huge yellow bulldozer, though it, too, was partly hidden beneath a cluster of Norfolk pines and what looked like a tangle of vines.

Weird.

Dropping lower now, the sea was multicoloured, the coral reefs beneath its surface visible like wavy patterns on a fine silk scarf. Images of herself and Keanu snorkelling in those crystal-clear waters, marvelling at the colours of the reef and the tiny fish that lived among the coral, flashed through her mind.

An ache of longing—for her carefree past, her childhood home—filled Caroline's heart, and she had to blink tears from her eyes.

How could she have stayed away so long?

Because Keanu was no longer here?

Or because she'd been afraid he might be…

'Are you okay?' Jill asked, and Caroline turned to her friend—her best friend—who, from seven hundred miles away, had heard the unhappiness in Caroline's voice just a short week ago and had told her she should go home.

Insisted on it, in fact, although Caroline suspected Jill had wanted to show off her new little plane, *and* her ability as a pilot.

'I'm fine, just sorry I've stayed away so long.'

'In recent times it's been because you were worried that

rat Steve would take up with someone else if you disappeared on him for even a week.'

The words startled Caroline out of her sentimental mood.

'Do you really think that? Do you believe I was that much of a doormat to him?'

Jill's silence spoke volumes.

Caroline sighed.

'I suppose he proved he didn't really care about me when he dropped me like a hot cake when the story about the Wildfire gold mine being in trouble appeared in the paper.'

But it was still upsetting—wounding...

Could the man who'd wooed Caroline with flowers, and gifts and words of love, who'd wrapped her in the security of belonging, really be the rat her friends thought him?

Had *she* really been so gullible?

'Maybe he *did* meet someone else,' Caroline answered plaintively. 'Maybe he was telling the truth.'

'That man wouldn't know the truth if it bit him on the butt,' Jill retorted, then fortunately stopped talking.

Caroline wasn't sure if it was because Jill was concentrating on her landing, or if she didn't want to hurt her friend even more.

Although she'd realised later—too late—that Steve *had* been inordinately interested in the mine her family owned...

The little plane bumped onto the tarmac, then rolled along it as Jill braked steadily.

'Strip's in good condition,' she said as she wheeled the craft around and stopped beside the shed that provided welcome to visitors to Wildfire Island.

But the shed needs repainting, Caroline thought, her elation at being home turning to depression because up close it was obvious the place was run-down.

Although the strip had been resurfaced.

Could things have come good?

No, her father had confirmed the mine was in trouble when she'd spoken to him about the article in the paper. Although all his time was spent in Sydney, working as a specialist physician at two hospitals, and helping care for Christopher, her twin, severely oxygen deprived at birth and suffering crippling cerebral palsy, the state of the mine was obviously worrying him.

He had been grey with fatigue from overwork and his fine face had been lined with the signs of continual stress from the hours he put in at work and worry over Christopher's health, yet with the stubborn streak common to all Lockharts he'd refused to even listen when she'd asked if she could help financially.

'Go to the island, it's where you belong,' he'd said gently. 'And remember the best way to get over pain is hard work. The hospital can always do with another nurse, especially now clinical services to the outer islands have expanded and we've had to cut back on hospital staff. Our existing staff go above and beyond for the island and the residents but there's always room for another pair of trained hands.'

Losing himself in work was what he'd done ever since her mother had died—died in his arms and left him with a premature but healthy baby girl and a premature and disabled baby boy to look after.

'Maybe whoever owns that very smart helicopter has an equally smart plane and needed the strip improved.'

Jill's comment brought Caroline out of her brooding thoughts.

'Smart helicopter? Our helicopters have always been run-of-the-mill emergency craft and Dad said we're down to one.'

But as she turned in the direction of Jill's pointing finger, she saw her friend was right. At the far end of the strip was a light-as-air little helicopter—a brilliant dragonfly of a helicopter—painted shiny dark blue with the sun picking out flashes of gold on the side.

'Definitely not ours,' she told Jill.

'Maybe there's a mystery millionaire your shady uncle Ian has conned into investing in the place.'

'From all I hear, it would take a billionaire,' Caroline muttered gloomily.

She'd undone her seat harness while they were talking and now opened the door of the little plane.

'At least come up to the house and have a cup of tea,' she said to Jill.

Jill shook her head firmly.

'I've got my thermos of coffee and sandwiches—like a good Girl Scout, always prepared. I'll just refuel and be off. It's only a four-hour flight. Best I get home to the family.'

Caroline retrieved her luggage—one small case packed with the only lightweight, casual summer clothes she owned. Her life in Sydney had been more designer wear— Steve had always wanted her to look good.

And I went along with it?

She felt her cheeks heat with shame as yet another of Steve's dominating characteristics came to mind.

Yes, she'd gone along with it and many other 'its', often pulling double shifts on weeknights to be free to go 'somewhere special' with him over the weekend.

The fact that the 'something special' usually turned out to be yet another cocktail party with people she either didn't know or, if she had known them, didn't particularly care for only made it worse.

But she'd loved him—or loved that he loved her…

Jill efficiently pumped fuel into the plane's tank, wiped her hands on a handy rag, and turned to her friend.

'You take care, okay? And keep in touch. I want phone calls and emails, none of that social media stuff where everyone can read what you're doing. I want the "not for public consumption" stuff.'

She reached out and gathered Caroline in a warm, tight hug.

'You'll be okay,' she said, and although the words were firmly spoken, Caroline heard a hint of doubt in them.

Dear Jilly, the first friend she'd made at boarding school so many years ago, now back in the cattle country of Western Queensland where she'd grown up, married to a fellow cattleman, raising her own family and top-quality beasts.

Caroline returned the hug, watched as Jill climbed back into the plane and began to taxi up the runway. She waved to the departing plane before turning to look around her.

Yes, the shed was a little run-down and the gardens weren't looking their best, but the peace that filled her heart told her she'd done the right thing.

She was home.

Bending to lift her suitcase, she was struck that something was missing. Okay, so the place wasn't quite up to speed, but where was Harold, who usually greeted every plane?

Harold, who'd told her and Keanu all the legends of the islands and given them boiled lollies so big they'd filled their mouths.

Her and Keanu...

Keanu...

She straightened her shoulders and breathed in the scented tropical air. That had been then and this was now.

Time to put the past—all the past—behind her, take control of her life and move on, as so many of her friends had advised.

And moving on obviously meant carrying her own suitcase up the track to the big house. Not that she minded, but it was strange that no one had met the plane, if only out of curiosity.

Had no one seen it come in?

Did no one care any more?

Or was Harold gone?

How old had he been?

She didn't like the tightening in her gut at the thought that someone who had been so much part of her life might have died while she'd been away...

Impossible.

Although all adults seemed old to children, she doubted Harold had been more than forty when she'd left—

The blast of a horn sent the past skittering from her mind, and she turned to see a little motorised cart—the island's main land transport—racing towards her from the direction of the research station.

'Are you the doctor?' the man driving it yelled.

'No, but I'm a nurse. Can I help?'

The driver pulled up beside her and gestured towards his passenger.

'We phoned the hospital. Someone said the doctor would come to meet us on the way. My mate was fine at first but now he's passed out, well, you can see...'

He gestured towards the man slumped in the back of the little dark blue vehicle. He had no visible injury—until she looked down and saw his foot.

Clad only in a rubber flip-flop, the foot had a nail punched right through beneath the small toe, and apparently into a piece of wood below his inadequate footwear.

Caroline slid in beside the man and put a hand on his chest. He was breathing, and his pulse— Yes, a bit fast but obviously it had been a very painful wound.

'I think we should get him up to the hospital as quickly as possible,' she said, as a figure appeared on the track they would take.

A figure she knew, although the intervening years had stretched him from an adolescent to a man—and for all her heart was bumping erratically in her chest, she certainly didn't know the man.

Caroline slid out of the cart and took the spare seat in front while Keanu, without more than a startled glance and a puzzled frown in her direction, took over in the back, fitting an oxygen mask to the man's face and adjusting the flow on the small tank he'd carried with him.

'Give me a minute to get some painkiller into him.'

Prosaic words but the deep, rich voice reverberated through Caroline's body—a man's voice, not a boy's…

This was Keanu?

Keanu was here?

She didn't know whether to hug him or hit him, but with witnesses around she could do neither. What she really wanted was to turn around and have another look at him, but the image of that first glimpse was burned into her brain.

Keanu the man.

Now grown into his burnished, almond-coloured skin, his grey eyes—his mother's eyes—strikingly pale beneath dark brows and hair.

Straight nose, tempting mouth, sculpted shoulders, abs visible beneath a tightly fitting polo shirt.

He was stunning.

More than that, he projected a kind of sexuality that would have every female within a hundred yards going weak at the knees just looking at him.

'Come back for a break from Sydney society?'

The cold wash of words obviously directed at her fixed the trembling knee thing, while the sarcasm behind them replaced it with anger.

She turned, chin tilted, refusing to reveal the hurt his words had caused.

'I'm a nurse, and I've come back to work, but I *am* surprised to see you here after the way you cut your connection to the islands so many years ago.'

Fortunately, as Caroline had just realised their driver was listening to this icy conversation with interest, they pulled up at the front of the hospital.

The patient was awake, obviously benefiting from the oxygen and the painkilling injection.

Keanu asked the driver to lend a hand, and the two of them eased the man out of the vehicle.

'Sling your arms around our shoulders and we'll help you in,' Keanu said, and Caroline guessed he was concentrating on the patient so he wouldn't have to look at her.

Or even acknowledge her presence?

What had happened?

What had she done?

Steely determination to not be hurt by him—or any man—ever again made her shut the door firmly on the past. Whatever had happened had been a long time ago, and she was a different person, had moved on, and was moving on again…

But walking behind Keanu, she couldn't *not* be aware of his presence. This man who'd been a boy she'd known so well was really something. Broad shoulders sloping down to narrow hips, but a firm butt and calf muscles that suggested not a workout in gym but a lot of outdoors exercise—he'd always loved running, said he felt free…

She was looking at his butt?

Best she get away, and fast.

But once they had the man on the deck in front of the hospital, Keanu turned back towards her.

'Well, if you're a nurse, don't just stand there. Come in and be useful. Hettie and Sam are on a clinic run to the outer islands and there's only an aide and myself on duty.'

He stood above her—loomed really—the disdain in his voice visible on his features.

And something broke inside her.

Was this really Keanu, her childhood friend and companion? Keanu, who had been gentle and kind, and had always taken care of her when she'd felt lost and alone?

Back then, his mother's mantra to him had always been 'Take care of Caroline', and Keanu, two years older, always had.

Which was probably why his disappearance from her life had hurt so deeply that for a while she'd doubted she'd get over it.

Head bent to hide whatever hurt might be showing on her face, she took the steps in one stride and followed the three men into the small but well-set-up room that she knew from the hospital plans doubled as Emergency and Outpatients.

Having helped lift the patient onto an examination table, the driver muttered something about getting back to work, and hurried through the door.

Which left her and Keanu…

Keanu, who was managing to ignore her completely while her body churned with conflicting emotions.

'Nail gun?' Keanu asked the patient as he examined the foot.

The patient nodded.

'Never heard of steel-capped workboots?' Keanu continued. 'I thought they were the only legal footwear on a building job.'

'Out here?' the man scoffed. 'Who's going to check?'

'Just hold his leg up for me, grasp the calf.'

An order to the nurse, no doubt, but even as he gave it Keanu didn't glance her way.

'No "please"?' Caroline said sweetly as she lifted the man's lower leg so Keanu could see just how far through the wood the nail protruded.

She must have struck a nerve with her words, for Keanu

looked up at her, his face unreadable, although she caught the confusion in his eyes.

So she wasn't the only one feeling this was beyond bizarre.

'Okay, let it down,' he said, the words another order.

Maybe she'd been wrong about the confusion.

Only then he added, 'Please,' and suddenly he was her old Keanu again, teasing her, almost smiling.

And the confusion *that* caused made her wish Jill hadn't taken off again so quickly. She had come here for peace and quiet, to heal after the humiliation of realising the man she'd thought had loved her had only been interested in her family money.

What was left of it.

'Here's a key.'

Keanu's fingers touched hers, and electricity jolted through her bones, shocking her in more ways than one. 'You'll find phials of local anaesthetic in the cupboard marked B, second shelf. Bring two—no, he's a big guy, maybe three—and you'll see syringes in there as well. Antiseptic, dressings and swabs are in the cupboard next to that one—it's not locked. Get whatever you think we'll need. I'm off to find a saw.'

The patient gave a shriek of protest but Keanu was already out of the room.

Slipping automatically into nurse mode, Caroline smiled as she unlocked the cupboard and found all she needed.

'He's not going to cut off your foot,' she reassured the man as she set up a tray on a trolley and rolled it over to the examination table. 'Hospitals have all manners of saws. We use diamond-tipped ones to cut through plaster when it has to come off, and we use adapted electric saws and drills in knee and hip replacement, though not here, of course. I'd say he's going to numb your leg from the calf down, then cut through the nail between your flip-flop and the wood. It's easier to pull a nail out of rubber and flesh than it is out of wood.'

Their patient didn't seem all that reassured, but Caroline, who'd found where the paperwork was kept, distracted him with questions about his name, age, address, any medication he was on, and, because she couldn't resist it, what he was doing on the island.

'Doing up the little places down on the flat,' was the reply, which came as Keanu returned with a small battery-powered saw and a portable X-ray machine.

'The research station,' he said, before Caroline could ask the patient what little places.

'They're doing up the research station when there's not enough money to keep the hospital running properly?'

The indignation in her voice must have been mirrored on her face, for Keanu said a curt, 'Later,' and turned his full attention to his patient.

After numbing the lower leg—Caroline being careful not to let her fingers touch Keanu's as she handed him syringes and phials—he explained to the patient what he intended doing.

'Nurse already told me that,' the man replied. 'Just get on with it.'

Asking Caroline to hold the wood steady, Keanu eased it as far as it would go from the flip-flop then bent closer to see what he was doing, so his head, the back of it, blocked Caroline's view. Not that she'd have seen much of the work, her eyes focussed on the little scar that ran along his hairline, the result of a long-ago exercise on her part to shave off all his hair with her grandfather's cut-throat razor.

Fortunately he must have been able to cut straight through the little bar of the nail, for he straightened before she could be further lost in memories.

Caroline dropped the wood into a trash bin and returned to find Keanu setting up a portable X-ray machine.

'We need to know if the nail's gone through bone,' he explained, helping her get back into nurse mode. 'And the picture should tell us if it's in a position that would have caused tendon damage.'

'Why does that make a difference?' Now he was pain-free—if only temporarily—the patient was becoming impatient.

'It makes the difference between pulling it out and cutting it out.'

'No cutting, just yank the damn thing out,' the patient said, but Keanu ignored him, going quietly on with the job of setting up the head of the unit above the man's foot.

Intrigued by the procedure—and definitely in nurse mode—Caroline had to ask.

'I thought the hospital had a designated radiography room,' she said, remembering protocols at the hospital where she'd worked that suggested wherever possible X-rays be carried out in that area, although the portables had many uses.

Keanu glanced up at her, his face once again unreadable.

'There is but I doubt you and I could lift him onto the table and with his leg already numb he's likely to fall if he tries to help us.'

Which puts me neatly back in my place, Caroline thought.

'Move back!'

Ignoring the peremptory tone, she stepped the obligatory two metres back from the head of the machine, watched Keanu don a lead apron—so protocols *were* observed here—and take shots from several angles.

That done, he wheeled the machine to the corner of the room, hung his apron over a convenient chair and checked the results on a computer screen.

'Come and look at this. What do you think?'

Assuming he was talking to her, not the immobile patient, she moved over to stand beside him—beside Keanu, who had been the single most important person in the world for her for the first thirteen years of her life. Important because, unlike her father, or even Christopher, he'd always been there for her—her best friend and constant companion.

Until he'd disappeared.

But this Keanu…

It was beyond weird.

Spooky.

And, oh, so painful…

'Well?' he demanded, and she forgot about the way Keanu was affecting her and concentrated on the images.

'By some miracle it's slipped between two metatarsals and though it's probably hit some ligament or tendon, because the bones are intact it shouldn't impact on the movement of the foot too much.'

'And don't look at me like that,' she muttered at him, after he'd shot yet another questioning glance her way. 'I *am* a trained nurse, and have been a shift supervisor in the ER at Canterbury Hospital.'

'I don't know how you found the time,' he said as he headed back to the patient.

She was about to demand what the hell he'd meant by that when she realised this was hardly the time or place to be having an argument with this man she didn't know.

Her friend had been a boy—was that the difference?

It certainly was part of it given the way her body was reacting to the slightest accidental touch…

'Okay, so now I need you to swab all around the nail then hold his foot while I try to yank the nail out. I'd prefer not to have to cut it out.'

Caroline put on new gloves, cleaned the areas above and beneath the foot, changed gloves again and got a firm grasp of the man's foot, ready to put all her weight into the task of holding on if the nail proved resistant.

But, no, it slid out easily, and as the wound was bleeding quite freely now, it was possible the risk of infection had been limited.

'Antibiotics and tetanus injections in the locked cupboard,' Keanu told her as he examined the wound in the patient's foot. 'And bring some saline and a packet of oral antibiotics as well. Everything's labelled as we get a lot of agency nurses coming out here for short stints. I'll use the saline to flush the wound before we dress it.'

He worked with quick, neat movements, cleaning the wound, putting the dressings on—usually, in her experience, a job left to a nurse—before administering the antibiotic and a tetanus shot. He even pulled a sleeve over the foot to keep the dressings in place and keep them relatively clean.

'Now all we have to do is get you back to your accommodation,' Keanu said. 'Keep off the foot for a couple of days and find your workboots before you go back on the job. If you don't have any you can phone the mainland and have some sent out on tomorrow's plane. Nurse Lockhart and I will help you out to a cart and I'll run you back down the hill.'

'I've got workboots,' the man said gruffly. 'And I'll phone my mate to come and get me, thanks. The foreman on the job doesn't like strangers on the site.'

'Strangers on the site? What site? What's happening at the research station, Keanu?'

He touched her on the arm.

'Leave it,' he said quietly, and the touch, more than his words, stopped her questions.

Since when had her body reacted to a casual touch from Keanu's hand?

It was being back on the island...

It was seeing him again…

Remembering the hurt…

Caroline closed her eyes, willing the tumult of emotions in her body to settle. She was here to heal, to find herself again, but she was also here to work.

She cleaned up, dropping soiled swabs into a closed bin marked for that purpose and the needles into a sharps box. Their patient was now sitting on the examination table, chatting to Keanu about, she found as she edged closer, fishing.

Well, it wasn't something she wanted to discuss right now, and as she needed time to sort out her reactions to seeing Keanu again, she slipped away, heading back down the track to the airstrip to collect her suitcase.

She could walk up to the house on the path behind the hospital and so avoid seeing the source of her confusion again. And once she was up at the house—home again— she could sort things out in her head—and possibly in her body—and…

And what?

Make things right between them?

She doubted that could ever happen. He had disappeared without a word, returned her letters unopened.

But now she'd have to work with him. Was she supposed to behave as if the life they'd shared had never happened?

As if his disappearance from it hadn't hurt her so badly she'd thought she'd never recover?

Impossible.

She'd reached the airstrip and grabbed her case by the time she'd thought this far and as further consideration of the problem seemed just that—impossible—she put it from her mind and started up the track, feeling the moisture in the air, trapped by the heavy rainforest on each side, wrap around her like a security blanket.

She was home, that was the main thing.

The track from the strip to the big house led up the hill behind the hospital and staff villas.

Staff villas?

Keanu.

Forget Keanu!

For her sanity's sake, she needed to work—she'd already sat around feeling sorry for herself for far too long as a result of another desertion.

And another nurse would always come in handy on the island even if they couldn't afford to pay her. She had her own place to live and some money Steve hadn't known about tucked away in the bank.

And wasn't this what she and Keanu had always planned to do?

He would become a doctor, she a nurse, and they'd return to Wildfire to run a hospital on the island. As children, they'd shared a picture book with a doctor and a nurse that had led to this childhood dream. Had it seemed more important because they had both lost a parent who possibly could have been saved if medical aid had been closer?

Half-orphans, they'd called themselves...

But as she hadn't existed for Keanu once he and his mother had left the island permanently, seeing him here, *and* seeing him carrying out *his* part of their dream, had completely rattled her.

Trudging up the track, she shook her head in disbelief at his sudden reappearance in her life, especially now when all she wanted to do was throw herself into work as an antidote to the pain of Steve's rejection.

Could she throw herself into work with Keanu around? Even seeing him that one time had memories—images—of their shared childhood flashing through her head.

Helen, his mother, had died not long after leaving the island. Caroline's father had passed on that information many years ago, but he'd offered no explanation the year

Caroline had found out she wouldn't be going to the island for her holidays as Helen and Keanu had left and there'd been no one to care for her.

And despite her grief at Helen's loss, she'd felt such anger against Keanu for not letting her know they were leaving, for not keeping in touch, for not telling her of his mother's death himself, that she'd shut him out of her mind, the hurt too deep to contemplate.

'I'll take that.'

Keanu's voice came from behind her, deep and husky, and sent tremors down her spine, while her fingers, rendered nerveless by his touch, released her hold on the case.

Why *had* he come back?

And why now?

But it was he who asked the question.

'Why did you come back?'

Blunt words but something that sounded like anger throbbed through them—anger that fired her own in response.

'It is my home.'

'*One* of your homes,' he reminded her. 'You have another perfectly comfortable one in Sydney with your father and your brother—your twin. How *is* Christopher?'

She spun towards him, sorry she didn't still have the suitcase to swing at his legs as she turned.

'How dare you ask that question? As if you care about my brother. People who care for others keep in touch. They don't just stop all communication. They don't send back letters unopened. I was twelve, Keanu, and suddenly someone who had been there for me all my life, someone I thought was my friend, was gone.'

Keanu bowed his head in the face of her anger, unable to bear the hurt in her eyes. Oh, he'd been angry at her reappearance, but that had been shock-type anger. He'd returned to Wildfire thinking her safely tucked away in Sydney, enjoying a busy social life.

Then, seeing her appear out of nowhere, so much unresolved anger and bitterness and, yes, regret had churned inside him he'd reacted with anger. But that anger should have been directed at another Lockhart. It was regret at the way he'd treated her—his betrayal of their friendship—that had added fuel to the fire.

Guilt…

And now he knew he'd hurt her again.

He'd learned to read Caro's hurt early. He'd first read it in a three-year-old looking forward to a visit from her daddy, the visit suddenly cancelled because of one thing or another.

Usually Christopher's health, he remembered now.

Throughout their childhood, she'd suffered these disappointments, a trip back to her Sydney home put off indefinitely because Christopher had chicken pox and was infectious. Going back to Sydney at ten when her adored grandmother had died, and learning it would be to boarding school because her father worked long hours and Christopher's carers could not take care of her as well…

'I'm sorry,' he said, apologising for all the hurts she'd suffered but knowing two words would never be enough.

'I don't want your "sorry" now, Keanu. I'm here, you're here, and we'll be working together, so we'll just both have to make the best of it.'

'You're serious about working in the hospital?'

Had he sounded astounded that she glared at him then turned away and stalked off up the path?

He followed her, taking in the shape of Caroline all grown up—long legs lightly tanned, hips curving into a neat waist, and long golden hair swinging from a high ponytail—swinging defiantly, if hair could be defiant.

The realisation that he was attracted to her came slowly.

Oh, he'd felt a jolt along his nerves when they'd accidentally touched, and his heart had practically somersaulted when he'd first set eyes on her, but surely that was remnants of the 'old friends' stuff.

And the attraction would have to be hidden as, apart from the fact that he was obviously at the very top of her least favourite people list, he was, as far as he knew, still married.

Not that he could blame Caro—for the least favourite people thing, not his marriage.

They'd both been sent to boarding school while still young, she to a school in Sydney, he to one in North Queensland, but the correspondence between them had been regular and intimate in the sense that they'd shared their thoughts and feelings about everything going on in their lives.

Then he and his mother had been forced to leave the island and there had been no way he could cause his mother further hurt by keeping in touch with Caroline.

She was a Lockhart after all.

A *Lockhart*!

He caught up with her.

'Look, no matter how you feel about me, there are things you should know.'

She turned her head and raised an eyebrow, so, taking that as an invitation, he ventured to speak.

'There's your uncle, Ian, for a start.'

Another quick glance.

'You must have known he came here, that your father had left him in overall charge of the mine after the hospital was finished and he, your father, that is, was doing more study and couldn't get over as often.'

She stopped suddenly, so he had to turn back, and standing this close, seeing the blue-green of her eyes, the dark eyebrows and lashes that drew attention to them, the curve of pink lips, the straight, dainty nose, his breath caught in his chest and left him wondering why no one had ever come up with an antidote for attraction.

Cold blue-green eyes—waiting, watchful…

'So?'

Demanding…

Keanu shifted uneasily. As a clan the Lockharts had always been extraordinarily close to each other and even though Ian was the noted black sheep, Caroline's father had still given him a job.

'Ian apparently had gambling debts before he came— a gambling addiction—but unfortunately even on a South Sea island online gambling is available. From all I heard he never stopped gambling but he wasn't very good at it. Eventually he sacked Peter Blake, the mine manager your father had employed, and took whatever he could from the mine—that's why it's been struggling lately and your father's having to foot a lot of the hospital bills. Ian stopped paying the mine workers, closed down the crushers and extractors and brought it to all but a standstill.'

He paused, although he knew he had to finish.

'Then he ran away. No one knows for certain when he went but it was very recently. One day his yacht was in the harbour at the mine and the next day it was gone.'

Blue-green eyes met his—worried but also wary.

'Grandma always said he was no good,' she admitted sadly. '"In spite of the fact he's my son, he's a bad seed," she used to say, which, as a child, always puzzled me, the bad-seed bit.'

He heard sadness in Caroline's words but she seemed slightly more relaxed now, he could tell, so he took a deep breath and finished the woeful tale.

'The trouble is, Ian's damaged the Lockhart name. I don't know how people will view your return.'

'What do you mean, view my return?'

Her confusion was so obvious he wanted to give her a hug.

Bad idea.

He put out his hand and touched her arm, wanting her calm enough to understand what he was trying to tell her. Though touching her was a mistake. Not only did fire flood his being, but she pulled away so suddenly she'd have fallen if he hadn't grabbed her.

And let her go very swiftly.

'Lockharts have been part of M'Langi history since they first settled on Wildfire,' he said gently. 'Your grandfather and father helped bring prosperity and health facilities to the islands and were admired for all they did. But Ian's behaviour has really tainted the name.'

He could see her confusion turning to anger and guessed she wanted to lash out at him—well, not at him particularly…or perhaps it was at him particularly, but she definitely wanted to lash out.

She turned away instead and trudged on up the slope, spinning back when she'd covered less than three feet to reach out and say, 'I'll take my bag now, thank you.'

Cool, calm and collected again—to outward appearances.

But he knew her too well not to know how deeply she'd been affected by his words. She'd never been a snob, never seen herself as different from the other island children with whom they'd attended the little primary school on Atangi, but she'd felt pride in the achievements of her family, justifiably so. To hear what he was telling her would be shattering for her.

But all he said was, 'I'll carry the bag, Caroline, and maybe, one day soon, we can sit down and talk—maybe find our friendship again.'

In reply, she stepped closer, grabbed her bag and stormed away, marching now, striding, hurrying away from him as fast as she could.

And was it his imagination, or did he hear her mutter, 'As if!'?

CHAPTER TWO

KEANU RUSSELL WALKED swiftly back down the track. He probably wasn't needed but the hospital was so short-staffed someone had to be there. The situation at the hospital was worse than he'd imagined when, alerted by the elders on Atangi, the main island of the group, he'd come back.

He touched the tribal tattoo that encircled the muscle of his upper arm, the symbol of M'Langi—of his belonging.

'Come home, we need you.'

That had been the extent of the elders' message, and as the islanders—with help from Max Lockhart—had paid for his high school and university education, he'd known he owed it to them to come.

He'd tried to contact Max before he'd left Australia but had been unable to get on to him. Apparently, Max's son, Christopher, had had a serious lung infection and Max had been with him in the ICU.

Trying the hospital here instead, Vailea, the hospital's housekeeper, had answered the phone and told him the islands—and the hospital in particular—were in big trouble.

'That Ian Lockhart, he's no good to anyone,' Vailea had told him. 'Max has been paying for the hospital out of his own money, because the mine is run-down and any money it does make, that rotten Ian takes.'

There was a silence as Keanu digested this, then Vailea added, 'We need you here, Keanu.'

'Why didn't *you* call me? Tell me this? Why leave it to the elders?'

There was another long pause before Vailea said, 'You've been gone too long, Keanu. I did not know how to tell you. I thought with me asking, you might not come, but with the elders—'

She broke the connection but not before he'd heard the tears in her voice, and he sat, staring at the phone in his hand, guilt flooding his entire being.

M'Langi was his home, the islanders his people, and he had stayed away because of his anger, and his mother's inner torment—caused by a Lockhart...

But if he was truly honest, he'd stayed away because he didn't want to face the memories of his happy childhood, or his betrayal of his childhood friend.

But home he was, and so aghast at the situation that memories had had no time to plague him. Although some-times when he walked through the small hospital late at night he remembered a little boy and even smaller girl holding hands on about the same spot, talking about the future when he would be a doctor and she would be a nurse and they would come back to the island and work in the hospital her father had, even then, been planning to build.

Okay, so the ghost of Caroline did bother him—had bothered him even as he'd married someone else—but there was enough work to do to block her out most of the time.

Or had been until she'd arrived in person. Not only ar-rived but apparently intended to work here.

Not that she wasn't needed...

The nurse they had been expecting to come in on the next day's flight had phoned to say her mother was ill and she didn't know when she might make it. Then Maddie Haddon, one of their Fly-In-Fly-Out, or FIFO doctors, had phoned to say she wouldn't be on the flight either—some mix-up with her antenatal appointments.

Sam Taylor, the only permanent doctor, was doing a clinic flight to the other islands, with Hettie, their head nurse—another permanent. They didn't know of the latest developments but as Keanu himself had come as a FIFO and intended staying permanently whether he was paid or not, he could cover for Maddie.

And, presumably, Caroline could cover for the nurse.

Caroline.

Caro.

He had known how hurt she would have been when he'd cut her out of his life, but his anger had been stronger than his concern—his anger and his determination to do nothing more to hurt his already shattered mother.

Caroline discovered why Harold hadn't met the plane. He was in the front garden of the house, arguing volubly with his wife, Bessie. It had been Caroline's great-grandfather, autocratic old sod that he must have been, who'd insisted that all the employees working in the house and grounds take on English names.

'You come inside and help me clean,' Bessie was saying.

'No, I have to do the yard. Ian will raise hell if the yard's not done, not that I believe he's coming back.'

Watching them, Caroline felt a stirring of alarm that they had grown old, although age didn't seem to be affecting their legendary squabbles.

'Nor do I but someone is coming. Some other visitor. We saw the plane on a day when planes don't usually come, and anyway it was too small to be one of our planes.'

'Might be for the research station. Plenty of people coming and going there,' Harold offered, but Bessie was going to have the last word.

'In that case you don't need to do the yard.'

Caroline decided she couldn't stand behind an alle-mande vine, wild with shiny green leaves and brilliant yellow trumpet flowers, eavesdropping any longer.

'Bessie, Harold, it's me, Caroline!'

She passed the bush and came into view, expecting to be welcomed like a prodigal son—or daughter in her case—but to her utter bewilderment both of them burst into tears.

Eventually they recovered enough from their shock to rush towards her, arms held out.

'Oh, Caroline, you have come back. Now we have you *and* Keanu back where you belong, everything will be good again.'

Wrapped in a double, teary hug, Caroline couldn't answer.

Not that she would have been able to. Although she knew he was here—knew only too well—hearing Keanu's name knocked the breath out of her. But it had been the last part—about everything being good again—that had been the bigger shock.

But it also gave her resolve. If the trouble was so bad the islanders thought she, whom they'd always considered a helpless princess, could help, things *must* be bad.

She eased out of their arms and straightened up. Of course she had to help. She didn't know how, but she certainly would do everything in her power to save the islanders' livelihood and keep much-needed medical care available to them.

Enough of the doormat.

M'Langi was her home.

'But why are you working in the house, Bessie? What happened to the young woman Dad appointed after Helen left?'

With Keanu, a voice whispered, but she had no time for whispering voices right now.

'That was Kari but from the time that Ian got here we

thought it would be better if she kept her distance,' Bessie explained. 'Ian is a bad, bad man for áll he's your family. In the end I said I'd do the housework. I mind Anahera's little girl too, but she's no trouble, she plays with all your toys and loves your dolls, dressing and undressing them.'

Caroline smiled, remembering her own delight in the dolls until Keanu had told her it was girl stuff and she had to learn to learn to make bows and arrows and to catch fish in her hands.

'Anahera?' she asked, as the name was vaguely familiar.

'Vailea, her mother, worked as the cook at the research station while we were caretakers there. But there's all kinds of funny stuff going on there too, so now she's housekeeper at the hospital and Anahera—she's a bit older than you and went to school on the mainland; her grandmother lived there—well, she's a nurse here so I mind her little one.'

It was hard to absorb so much information at once, so Caroline allowed herself to be led up to the house, where a very small child with dark eyes, olive skin and a tangle of golden curls was lining up dolls in a row on the cane lounge that had sat on the veranda for as long as Caroline could remember.

The cane lounge, potted palms everywhere, a few cane chairs around a table, once again with a smaller pot in the middle of it, and the swing she and Keanu had rocked in so often—*this* was coming home...

'This is Hana,' Bessie said, leading the little girl forward. 'Hana, this is Miss Caroline. She lives here.'

Caroline knelt by the beautiful child, straightening one of the dolls.

'Just Caroline will do,' she said, 'or even Caro.'

Caro.

No one but Keanu had ever called her Caro, but now wasn't the time to get sentimental over Keanu, for all he looked like a Greek god, and had sent shivers down her spine just being close to him.

She was here to…

What?

She'd come because she was unhappy, seeking sanctuary in the place she'd loved most, but now she was here?

Well, she was damned if she was going to let things deteriorate any further.

But first she had to find out exactly how things stood, and whether whoever ran the hospital would give her a job, and most importantly of all right now, she had to find the steel in her inner self to work with Keanu…

'Are you being paid, Bessie?' she asked, thinking she had to set her own house in order first.

Bessie studied her toes then shook her dark, curly hair.

'Anahera pays me for looking after Hana, but it's been a while since Harold got a wage.'

Caroline was angry. She knew their fondness for the Lockhart family and gratitude for what her father had done for the islands would have kept them doing what they could whether they were paid or not.

Knew also that the couple wouldn't be starving. Like all the islanders, and many people she knew on acreage on the mainland, they had their own plot of land around their bure—the traditional island home—and Harold would grow vegetables and raise a few pigs and chickens, but that didn't make not paying them right.

'Well, now I'm here we'll shut off most of the rooms and I'll just use my bedroom, bathroom and the kitchen. I can pay you to keep them clean and I'll vacuum through the rest of the place once a fortnight.'

Bessie began to mutter about dust, but Caroline waved away her complaint.

'Lockharts have been eating dust since the mine began,' she said, 'so a little bit on the floor of the closed rooms doesn't matter. And now,' she announced, 'I'm going down to the hospital to ask whoever runs it for a job. Even if they can't pay me, they can surely find me something to do.'

She left her case and headed back down the way she'd come. Work would give her the opportunity to find out what was going on. Even small hospitals were hotbeds of gossip.

Although…

Of course she could work with Keanu. She didn't know the man he'd become so she'd just treat him like any other colleague.

Male colleague.

Friendly, but keeping her distance…

Definitely keeping her distance, given how the accidental touches had affected her…

Lost in her muddled thoughts, she was halfway to the hospital when she remembered the only people there had been Keanu and an aide. What had he said? Hettie and Sam were on a clinic run? Caroline knew the hospital ran weekly clinics on the other inhabited islands of the group and today must have been one of those days.

That was probably the only reason Keanu had accepted her help with the injured man earlier.

She walked back up the hill, wondering why she'd thought returning to the island was such a good idea.

Wondering how things had gone so wrong, not only with the island but between herself and Keanu.

Had she judged him too harshly?

Refused to accept he might have had a good reason for stopping communication between them?

But surely they'd been close enough for him to have given her a reason—an explanation?

Hadn't they?

Totally miserable by the time she reached the house, she

went through to her old bedroom and unpacked the case that either Bessie or Harold had left there.

Then, as being back in her old room brought nostalgia with it, she slowly and carefully toured the house.

Built like so many colonial houses in those days, it had a wide veranda with overhanging eaves around all four sides of it. She started there, at the front, looking down at the hospital and beyond it the airstrip, and onto the flat ground by the beach, and although she couldn't see the research station, she knew it was there, sheltered beneath huge tropical fig trees and tall coconut palms.

As she knew the village was down there, on the eastern shore, nestled up against the foothills of the plateau. The village had been built on land given by her father, after the villagers on another island had lost their homes and land in a tsunami.

Now some of the villagers worked in the mine and at the hospital, and worshipped in the little white church they'd built on a rocky promontory between the village and the mine. A chapel built to celebrate their survival.

She knew the beach was there as well, but that too was hidden, although as she turned the corner and looked across the village she saw the strip of sand and the wide lagoon enclosed by the encircling coral.

On a clear day, from here and the back veranda, she'd have been able to see most of the islands that made up the M'Langi group, but today there was a sea haze.

The western veranda formed the division between the main house and the smaller copy of it, an annexe where Helen and Keanu had lived.

No way was she going there now, although their home had been as open to her as hers had been to Keanu.

This time she entered the house through the back door, through the kitchen with its different pantries opening off it and the huge wooden table where she and Keanu had eaten breakfast and lunch.

The pantries had provided great places for hide and seek, although Grandma's cook had forever been shooing them out, afraid they'd break the precious china and crystal stored in them.

Caroline opened the door of one—empty shelves where the crystal had once reflected rainbows in the light.

The sight sent her hurrying to the dining room, on the eastern side of the main hall. Looking up, she saw with relief that the chandelier still hung above the polished dining table.

Grandma had loved that table *and* the grandeur of the chandelier. She had insisted Caroline, Keanu and Helen join her there for dinner every evening, the magic crystals of the chandelier making patterns on the table's highly polished surface.

Helen would report on anything that needed doing around the house, and talk to Grandma about meals and what needed to be ordered from the mainland to come over on the next flight.

Grandma would quiz Keanu and Caroline about their day at school—what they'd learned and had they done their homework before going out to play.

Ian might have sold her grandmother's precious crystal to cover his gambling debts but at least he'd left the chandelier.

He must have been desperate indeed to have packed the delicate objects before sending them out on the boat that made a weekly visit to the harbour at Atangi.

Before or after he'd started skimming money from the mine?

Taking away the livelihood of the workers?

Shame that she could be related to the man brought heat to her cheeks, but what was done was done.

Unless?

Could she do something to help set things to rights?

Refusing to be waylaid, she continued with her exploration. Next to the dining room was the big entertaining room Grandma had always called the Drawing Room—words Caroline still saw in her mind with capital letters. Here, at least, things remained the same. The furniture, the beautiful old Persian carpets—Ian couldn't have known they were valuable.

But the elegant, glass-fronted cabinets were empty. Grandma's precious collection of china—old pieces handed down to her by *her* mother and grandmother—was gone.

That was when tears started in Caroline's eyes. Ian had not only stolen physical things, he'd stolen her memories, memories of sitting on the floor in front of the cabinet while Grandma handed her one piece at a time, telling her its history, promising they would be hers one day.

That she'd lost them didn't matter, but the treachery of Ian selling things he knew had been precious to his mother turned her tears to anger.

Taking a deep breath, she moved on into Grandma's sitting room.

The little desk she'd used each day to write to friends was there, and Caroline could feel the spirit of her grandmother, the woman who, with Helen, had brought her up until Grandma's death when Caroline was ten.

Opening off the wide passage on the other side were large, airy bedrooms, all with wide French doors and folding shutters that led onto the veranda. The filmy lace curtains still graced the insides of the windows, although they were beginning to look drab.

Grandma's was the first room, the huge four-poster bed draped with a pale net, the faint scent of her presence lingering in the air. There'd always been flowers in Grandma's room, as there had been on the dining-room table and the cabinets in the drawing room...

Leaving her exploration, she hurried out into the garden, minding the thorns on the bougainvillea as she pulled off a couple of flower stems, then some frangipani, a few yellow allemande flowers, some glossy leaves, and white daisies.

Back inside she found vases Ian must have considered too old and cracked to fetch a decent price. She filled them with water and carried them, one by one, into the three rooms where flowers had always stood.

Soon she'd do more—head into the rainforest for leaves and berries and eventually have floral tributes to Grandma that would rival the ones she used to make.

But there was still half a house to explore.

Her father's room was next, unchanged although the small bed beside her father's big one reminded Caroline of the rare times Christopher had come to the island. The visits hadn't lasted long, but she and Keanu had always shared their adventures with him. They would put him in his wheelchair and show him all their favourite places, probably risking his life when they wheeled him down the steep track to Sunset Beach.

The next room must have been Ian's, then three smaller, though still by modern-day standards large, rooms—hers in the middle.

But as she poked her head into Ian's room it was obvious he hadn't been living there as the furniture was covered in dust sheets that seemed to have been there for ever.

'He lived in the guesthouse.'

Bessie had come in and now stood beside Caroline, looking into the empty, rather ghostly room.

The guesthouse was off the back veranda opposite Helen and Keanu's suite of rooms, but detached and given privacy by a screen of trees and shrubs.

'I don't think I'll bother looking there,' she said to Bessie. 'It was about the only place on the island Keanu and I weren't allowed to play so there'd be no memories.'

She was back on the front veranda when she heard the *whump-whump-whump* of a helicopter.

Now she could go down to the hospital and ask for a job.

Right now before she'd let her doubts about working with Keanu solidify in her head.

Or perhaps tomorrow when she'd worked on a strategy to handle working with him…

He had to go up to the house and make peace with Caro, Keanu decided, not skulk around down here at the hospital.

Sam and Hettie would employ her, that much was certain, so he would be working with her. But doctor-nurse relationships needed trust on both sides and although all his instincts told him to run for his life, he knew he wouldn't.

Couldn't.

M'Langi was more important than these new and distinctly uncomfortable reactions to Caro. Finding out what had been happening and trying to put things right—that was what the elders expected of him.

So he was here, and she was here, and…

He sighed, then began to wonder just why she was here. He'd never totally lost touch with what Caro was up to, being in contact with her father all through his student years, asking, oh, so casually, how she was doing.

And friends from the islands, staying at the Lockharts' Sydney house on a visit or while studying, would pass on information. So now he thought about it, he'd known she'd studied nursing, because he'd smiled at the time to think both of them were fulfilling at least the beginning of that childhood promise.

But he'd never expected her to return to Wildfire to actually finish the job, especially as he'd known a little of the life she'd been leading. Known from the Sydney papers he would buy up in Cairns, for the sole purpose, he realised, of torturing himself.

He might pretend he'd bought them for the business section, which was always more comprehensive than the one in the local paper, but, if so, why did he turn to the social pages first, hoping for a glimpse of Caro—a grown-up, beautiful Caro—usually on the arm of a too-smooth-looking bloke called Steve, to whom she was, apparently, 'almost' engaged.

What the hell did 'almost' mean?

It couldn't have been jealousy that had made him feel so bad—after all, he'd been the one who'd not almost but definitely married someone else. Someone he'd thought he'd loved because she'd brought him out of the lingering misery of his mother's death, his loneliness and his homesickness for the island.

So kind of, in a way, he'd betrayed Caro not once—in disappearing from her life—but twice, although that wasn't really true as trysts made between twelve-and fourteen-year-olds didn't really count.

Did they?

It was all this confusion—the unresolved issues inside him—that was making him angry, and somehow the anger had made her its target.

Which was probably unfair.

No, it was definitely unfair.

Especially as she was obviously unhappy. He'd put that down to her seeing him again, which would be natural after the way he'd behaved towards her.

So maybe he should stay well out of her way.

Except he'd always hated it when Caro was unhappy. And if he'd caused or even contributed to that unhappiness, which he must have, cutting her off the way he had so long ago, then shouldn't he do something about it?

At least see if they could regain a little of their old friendship.

Friendship?

When one glimpse of the grown-up Caro had sent his pulses racing, his entire body stirring in a most un-friend-like manner?

Not good for a man who was probably still married...

On top of which, he was torn between two edicts of his mother. The childhood one, always spoken when the two of them as children had left the house, plainly spoken and always understood: take care of Caroline.

Then, as his mother had been dying from pancreatic cancer that had appeared from nowhere and killed her within six weeks, while he, a doctor could do nothing to save her. *Then* she had *cursed* the Lockharts...

Well, Ian Lockhart anyway.

Anyway, wasn't he beyond superstitions like curses?

He shook his head to clear the memories and useless speculation, checked the few patients they had in the hospital, then let out a huge sigh of relief when he heard the helicopter returning.

He almost let himself hope it was bringing in a difficult case, something to distract him from the endlessly circling thoughts in his head.

Hettie and Sam had left the hospital's makeshift ambulance down near the helicopter pad so Keanu walked down to the airstrip, not really wishing for a patient but ready to help unpack anything they might have brought back. And it would be best to break the news about the FIFO nurse and Maddie not coming now, rather than leaving it until the morning.

Would he tell them about Caroline's arrival?

He'd have to at least mention it.

Sam would be only too delighted to have an available nurse.

And he would be doomed to work with the woman he didn't really know but had been instantly attracted to in a way he'd never felt before.

It was because of the old friendship. The attraction thing. It had to be, but with any luck, after the way he'd treated her, she'd want to have as little to do with him as possible.

He was almost at the helicopter now, and could see Sam and Jack Richards, the pilot, lifting out a stretcher.

Good! That means work to do, Keanu thought, then realised how unkind it was to be wishing someone ill. But it was only when he saw the patient that he felt a flush of shame at his thoughts. It was old Alkiri, from the island of Atangi, the elder who had been one of his and Caro's favourite people and true mentor when they had been young.

He moved closer and greeted the elder in his native language, touching the old man's shoulder in a gesture of respect.

Even through the oxygen mask, Keanu could see the blue tinge on their patient's lips and he wondered just how old Alkiri might be.

'He had a fall, perhaps a TIA as apparently he'd been falling quite a lot recently.'

TIA—transient ischemic attack—often a precursor to a full-blown stroke. Had Alkiri been putting these falls down to old age? He was a private man, unlikely to seek help unless he really needed it. Yet, as Caroline's grandfather's boatman, he had not only lived here at Wildfire but had taken two small children under his wing. It was he who had taken them and the village children to and from the school on Atangi, teaching them things about the islands, and life itself, that to Keanu were as important as the learning he'd had at school.

He should tell Caro Alkiri was—

He stopped the thought before it went any further. It had been automatic for he knew she'd loved the old man as much as he had—and probably still would...

But he was no longer the boy who'd run through the house, calling for his friend to pass on a bit of news.

And she was no longer the girl he'd always wanted to find so he could tell—

They strapped the stretcher into the converted jeep, especially modified for just that reason, then Jack and Hettie rode back to the hospital, Sam walking with Keanu to check on any news and pass on information from the clinics on the other islands.

The scent of a nearby frangipani hung in the air, but today such a reminder that he was home didn't soothe Keanu as it had on other days, on other such walks with Sam, or Hettie or whoever had done the clinic run.

He gave Sam the news that neither Maddie nor the FIFO nurse would be arriving the next day, assured Sam he was happy to work full time, then hesitated.

'More?' Sam asked quietly.

'There *is* a nurse,' Keanu answered, and something in his voice must have alerted Sam.

'She's a problem? Drinker? Chain smoker who'll insist on cigarette breaks? Axe murderer?'

'She's a Lockhart,' Keanu answered, and watched as Sam smiled and shook his head.

'That doesn't make her a bad nurse, Keanu. I assume she's Max's daughter, the girl you grew up with. And don't look at me like that—nothing stays secret on this island for long.'

Sam stopped walking and turned towards Keanu, his usually smiling face set in a frown.

'Are you saying you can't work with her?'

'Of course not,' Keanu responded, possibly too quickly. 'But the Lockhart name isn't held in much regard here at the moment. I was wondering about the patients.'

'Of course you were.'

Sam smiled again.

'Considering all the good Max Lockhart and his parents and grandparents before him have done for the islands, I doubt the one bad apple will have totally ruined the name. I do hope not, because we need her. But speaking of Ian, Hettie and I discovered he'd stopped in at Raiki after he left here and took not only the locked box of drugs we kept in the clinic there, but also the clinic nurse.'

'Why on earth?' Keanu had trouble taking in this information. 'Drugs, maybe—he's on a boat, could have injuries and presumably anything he doesn't use he'll sell—but the nurse? I assume she went willingly.'

'Apparently so, but it leaves Raiki without a nurse. The drugs we can replace, but she was one of the first nurses trained when Max set up the programme to help any islanders wanting to do nursing. Most of them lived in his house in Sydney while they were at university, but she was one of the few who came back here to work.'

'But the others will be helping people even if it's not here,' Keanu pointed out, mainly to cover the stab of guilt he'd felt at Sam's statement. It had reminded him that he, too, hadn't come back—well, not until he had been reminded of his duty...

'So, when do I get to meet her?' Sam asked.

'I imagine she'll come down in the morning. She did help out soon after she arrived earlier today when we had a bloke come up from the research station with a nail from a nail gun in his foot. It wasn't much of a test of nursing but she seemed to know what she was doing.'

Sam smiled again before walking on.

'Poor girl!' he said. 'Already damned with faint praise.'

Poor girl indeed, Keanu muttered to himself. If she was still a girl everything would be okay.

Or would it?

She'd been nothing more than a girl when he'd hurt her and for all he'd told himself she wouldn't miss his letters, and would probably be relieved not to have to write back, given all the friends she would have made at school, he'd never quite believed it.

'I could take you up to the house and introduce you this evening if you like,' he offered.

Sam studied him for a minute.

'Let's just wait for her to come to us,' he suggested, then he grinned. 'And let's hope she's early as apparently she'll have to start work straight away.'

CHAPTER THREE

A BEAUTIFUL YOUNG woman with long, lustrous, dark hair piled up beneath a dodgy-looking nurse's cap, and wearing what was apparently a uniform of green tunic and green three-quarter-length pants greeted Caroline with a smile and, 'Can I help you?'

'I'm looking for Sam,' Caroline explained.

'Rather you than me,' the woman replied. 'He's in the little room he calls his office, probably setting fire to the paperwork. Straight along the passage and on the left.'

Caroline turned to follow the directions.

'I'm Anahera, by the way, but everyone calls me Ana,' the dark-haired woman added.

Caroline turned back.

'Oh, I've met your daughter. She's adorable. I'm Caroline Lockhart.'

Caroline held out her hand but couldn't miss the hesitation or the look of wariness in Anahera's eyes before she took the proffered palm and shook it.

But 'Oh!' was all she said, turning back into the small ward behind her where Caroline could see four occupied beds.

Farther down the passage she found the room, knocked briefly then answered a peremptory 'Come in.'

'Caroline Lockhart, I presume?'

The good-looking man behind the desk looked up briefly from the paperwork he was shoving from one pile to another, then frowned down at it.

'Never become an administrator,' he muttered, pushing the lot back together into an untidy heap.

'Don't like paperwork?' Caroline asked, but she was smiling as she said it. There was something immensely likeable about this man.

'Who does? The problem is I'm already short on staff and I've still got to waste time doing blasted paperwork.'

'Can't you get the dog to eat it? Isn't that the classic homework excuse?' Caroline suggested, seeing the warm brown eyes of the Labrador lying on Sam's feet under the table.

Sam flashed her a grin.

'I did try that but the wretch keeps spitting it out. Hospital dogs are too well fed. But let me introduce you. This lazy, too-well-fed beast is Bugsy, Maddie Haddon's dog. Maddie is one of our FIFO doctors but rather than fly Bugsy back and forth she leaves him here. Unfortunately she can't make today's plane and as he usually knows when she's due in, he's decided I'm the best substitute for his owner.'

Sam paused and studied Caroline for a moment.

'I'm also a nurse short, and Keanu told me you were here. Want a job?'

'As long as it doesn't involve sorting that mess you've made of those papers you're shuffling. I can certainly help in other ways.'

Humour lit his eyes.

'Nice back massage? Rub my feet?'

'In your dreams!' Caroline retorted, deciding she quite liked this rather strange man.

'But I could fill in for your missing nurse,' Caroline

added, refusing to be beguiled by gleaming eyes. 'I'm a nurse and you're apparently one nurse short.'

'Keanu said you're a socialite.'

One more black mark against the man who'd hurt her so badly.

'Well, you may not have noticed but there's not that much social life around here, and a socialite without a social set is superfluous to requirements, while a nurse might just fill in for the one who isn't coming, if you're willing to give me a chance.'

Now she had his attention.

'Touchy, are you?' He looked her up and down. 'I suppose you have the right bits of paper—degree, references.'

'Right here,' she said, pulling the paperwork she'd grabbed and stuffed in her back pocket before leaving the house.

Caroline began to relax.

Well, not *relax* relax—that would never happen with Keanu somewhere near—but some of the tension she'd been feeling drained slowly out of her.

'It seems you've been away from the island for a long time,' Sam said, riffling through the papers but, she suspected, speed-reading every word. 'Why have you come back?'

'I don't think that's relevant but I did hear the island was in trouble.'

'And you thought coming here to nurse would cure things?'

Caroline shook her head.

'Boy, are you a grump! I didn't even know there'd be a nursing position available, although I had intended working here for nothing if necessary, but this place was my home—*is* my home—and I'll be damned if I'm going to sit back and let it fall apart without at least trying to find out what's been happening and what can be done to save it. My dad would be here as well, only he— Well, there's a family problem.'

Sam raised his head and looked at her.

'He's a great man, your father. He does the best he can. Lobbying for government support, fundraising. Ever since the mine stopped paying its promised share for the hospital, I think he's put his entire salary into it. I just do what I can.'

'So, do I get a job?'

Sam studied her a little longer.

'The nurse who was coming was a FIFO—Fly-In-Fly-Out—the term more commonly used in mining communities. It means you're on duty for two weeks then off for one, and you can take the flight to the mainland for that week off if you wish.'

'Which leaves you with only one nurse—Anahera—for a week?'

'Not really. The FIFOs overlap and we have another permanent. You haven't met Hettie yet—Henrietta de Lacey—only don't dare ever call her Henrietta, she'll lop off your head with the nearest implement. She's our head nurse and is permanent staff and she's the one you should be speaking to about this job, but she's doing another clinic run. It's not usual to do two in one week, but there's a lot to sort out. The clinic on Raiki is short of drugs, not to mention a nurse, so Hettie's gone out there to replace the drugs then scour the islands to see if she can get one of the nurses from another island to cover Raiki for a while. How are you in a helicopter?'

Caroline was wondering what had happened to both the drugs and the nurse from Raiki when she realised she'd been asked a question. She grinned at him.

'Do you mean can I fly one or do I throw up in one?'

'Definitely the latter. Pilots we have.'

'I'll be fine, but do nurses always do the clinics or do the doctors go out to the other islands as well?'

'Doctors too,' came the swift reply, although Caroline had already forgotten what she'd asked as she'd sensed a presence in the room behind her, and every nerve in her body told her it was Keanu.

'Sorry to butt in, boss.'

His deep voice reverberated around the room.

'But Alkiri, the old man you brought in from Atangi, is having difficulty breathing—I think his end is very near. Okay with you if I sit with him?'

Sam nodded, then turned to Caroline.

'If you want to start work now, go sit with Keanu. Just see Alkiri is propped up in a comfortable position and moisten his lips for him if he needs it. Turn his head a little—'

'So saliva can drain out,' Caroline finished for him. 'I *have* done this before, you know.'

Sam nodded again, then added softly, although they were already alone in the room, 'I'd like you there for Keanu. He's known the old man all his life. He's the elder who asked Keanu to come back to the islands. It will be hard for him.'

Caroline nodded.

'Alkiri would have known he was dying,' she murmured, remembering the uncanny sense the islanders seemed to have about death. 'Maybe he wanted Keanu by his side.'

She left the room to be with Alkiri and Keanu, though she doubted *he'd* take comfort from her presence.

Sitting on the opposite side of the bed from her childhood friend, she took the old man's dry hand, feeling bones as fragile as a bird's beneath the papery skin.

'It's Caroline,' she said very quietly. 'Do you remember teaching me to weave fish traps?'

To talk or not to talk to the dying was a much-argued topic, but Caroline thought Alkiri deserved to know she remembered, and perhaps to let his mind drift back to happy times he'd had with the two children.

'Then you'd take us out in your old boat to show us where to put them up against the reef.' Keanu took up the story equally quietly, but looking at him, Caroline wondered if the sadness in his eyes was not all caused by the elder's approaching death.

Caroline swabbed the saliva from the old man's mouth, while Keanu started a story about Alkiri's frustration at not being able to teach Caro to split a coconut properly.

'I still can't,' Caroline admitted, 'although they're everywhere in the city shops now and people are going crazy for coconut water.'

'I've been looking into that and have talked to the elders,' Keanu said quietly. 'Wondering if the craze for it might provide a viable source of income for the islanders. After all, it's not just the water but every bit of a coconut is used in one way or another. I've got an accountant who's done a lot of set-up work on new businesses looking at the figures.'

Her thoughts hadn't quite got that far but the splitting of coconuts had started her thinking that way.

She risked a glance towards him. Surely they were not still going to be able to read each other's thoughts, especially now, when her thoughts, since meeting him again, had been almost wholly taken up with how magnificent he looked.

Keanu was as fine a specimen of manhood as she'd ever seen, and although just looking at him generated unwelcome reactions in her body, she couldn't resist a sneaked glance now and then as she tried to analyse her reactions.

She turned her attention back to Alkiri, speaking quietly again, more memories tumbling into her head. Keanu offered some of his own, adding to hers—shared lives.

At some stage she heard a plane come in—bringing

stores but not the staff that had been expected, Caroline guessed. Then some time later it took off again. They talked on…

There were long silences between Alkiri's rattly breaths, some so long she feared their old friend had already died. Until suddenly he roused, opened his eyes and looked from one to the other, smiling.

'With both of you here, I am at peace. Please keep me here when I am gone. Wildfire was always my true home,' he whispered in a thin papery voice, and then the breathing did stop.

For ever.

Caroline couldn't bring herself to pull the sheet up over the old man's face. Very gently, she closed his eyes, and straightened the sheet across his body.

'*Can* we bury him here or would his family want him back on Atangi?' she asked, finally meeting Keanu's eyes across the bed.

Keanu shrugged, and, sensing the grief he was trying hard to hide she went to him, unable not to offer comfort to her old friend, and put her arm around his wide shoulders.

'Come on, let's have a cup of tea while we think about the arrangements.'

He walked with her, but blindly, although the fact that he was not aware of her didn't bother Caroline one bit. She was far too busy battling all the reactions just touching Keanu's body had caused in hers—hoping the deep breaths she was taking to suppress the weird emotions were going unnoticed by her companion.

But her heart raced, her head spun, and every nerve in her body tingled with excitement.

Ridiculous, she told herself. This was 'old friend' reaction and not sexual at all, although it *did* feel…

Sexual?

Vailea was in the kitchen. She took one look at Keanu's stricken face and pulled out a chair for him.

'I heard you were back,' she said, her voice cold enough to douse the fires just touching Keanu had set alight. 'Come to bring more trouble to us?'

'No, of course not. I've come to work.' Caroline tried to sound reassuring, but Vailea's words and attitude had stung.

What on earth had been going on? Was it more than Ian's poor management? Selling off the family heirlooms wouldn't have affected anyone outside the family, so what else had happened or was happening? What had Bessie said about the new housekeeper? Something about Ian...

'I've come to make Keanu a cup of tea,' she said as Vailea's eyes continued to study her, a malevolence Caroline couldn't understand clear within them.

'I'll take care of him,' the older woman snapped, and Caroline, only too pleased to escape the extremely uncomfortable atmosphere, left the kitchen.

'Boy, this is going to be fun,' she muttered to herself as she made her way out of the hospital.

Keanu could deal with Alkiri on his own—do whatever needed to be done. She was damned if she was going to stay around and be insulted. Once Hettie, the head nurse, returned later today and gave Caroline her roster, she could work out how best to avoid Vailea altogether.

Vailea *and* Keanu.

Although there was something about Vailea's reaction to her that seemed more personal than a general hatred of all Lockharts...

Keanu walked up to the house at six. He'd spent two hours talking to the elders on Atangi, making arrangements for Alkiri's funeral. The elders had agreed he could be buried on Wildfire and they would send over people to help with the practicalities and some cooks to prepare the food.

'Is there somewhere we can all gather?' the man he'd been speaking to had asked. 'I think the little church and its hall would be too small.'

Keanu thought of the big longhouse that had once been the centre of the research station and assured the elder that somewhere could be found. There was always the Lockhart house if nothing else worked out.

They settled on a service at ten in two days' time.

Now, given that they might need the house, he had to make peace with Caro, although he doubted he could ever explain his angry reaction to her arrival—far too complicated and quite unwarranted, really.

Caroline was sitting on the veranda, watching the sun sink into the sea, dropping below the western cliffs lit up with the brilliant fiery red that gave the island its name.

He took the steps three at a time in long, deliberate strides, then slumped down on the top one, not looking at her but out at the dying colours of the sunset.

'Why *did* you come back?' he asked, almost gently, although being this close to her had started all the physical reactions again, and the confusion of that made him feel...

Angry?

Not really, more unsettled...

'Why did you?' she countered.

'I was asked,' he said, trying desperately to pretend that this was just a conversation between two old friends. Which, of course, it was—wasn't it?

'The island was in trouble, the community was in trouble. It's my home and I love it. Of course, I had to come back.'

'And yet you ask me why I came? To tell you the truth,

I didn't know things were this bad until I got here. I just wanted—needed—to come home.'

'And now you're here?

She turned towards him, her eyes alight with determination.

'I have to find out what's been happening. How everything's gone so terribly wrong. Do you honestly believe the island means less to me than it does to you? That this isn't my community as well?'

Her gaze drifted back to the sunset, so he guessed there was a bit more to the answer than that. But whatever it was it had caused a break in her voice and he wanted more than anything in the world—more even than saving the livelihood and well-being of the islanders—to comfort her, to take her in his arms, hold her close, smell the Caro scent of her, and never let her go.

Like she'd want *that*!

He also wanted to ask her about Christopher. She hadn't answered earlier. But he knew it was too painful a subject to bring up when they were so estranged, so he stuck to practicalities.

'So, what do you think you can do?' he asked instead, his voice rougher than it should be as it scraped past the emotion in his throat.

'Find out what's been going on, for a start,' she said. 'All the predictions from the geologists showed the mine had many years to run. I don't doubt Ian's been embezzling the money it's been earning but it can't *just* be that.'

Keanu hid a smile. That sounded so like the young Caroline—his Caro—on the trail of some possible crime—suspected cruelty to some chickens being only one of her campaigns.

Memories were dangerous things…

Better to stick with the present and practicalities, discuss what facts he *did* know, although they were few enough.

'Did you know Ian leased out the research station?' he asked.

'He's leased the research station? Why on earth would he do that?'

'Money, why else! It had been run-down for a while. Fewer and fewer people using it. Then he somehow found this wealthy Middle Eastern guy who wants to set up an exclusive resort. The local residents are a bit uneasy about it, but heaven knows we need all the income and employment we can get.'

'Well, it explains the guy with the nail in his foot. Does my dad know?'

'I assumed he did but the negotiations certainly went through Ian, and no one here seems to know anything about it.'

'Dad would never have trusted Ian to negotiate, and he'd never have made a decision without consulting the elders. He sent Ian here mainly to keep him out of trouble. It's the way Dad feels about family. He thinks even the black sheep deserves a chance to redeem himself, but from all I'm hearing about our particular black sheep, it's impossible.'

She sighed then added, 'The guy with the nail in his foot—he's working there? Work's going on now?'

Keanu nodded. 'And has been for some time.'

'I want to have a look.'

'You can't. The whole place is fenced and gated. That patient yesterday wouldn't even let us drive him back down there. He had his mate come back to the hospital, remember?'

'But this is our home! We can go wherever we like.'

Keanu hid a smile. This was Caro at her most imperious. And hearing her, hearing the old Caro sent a piercing pain through his chest.

'You want to argue with the guards? They'll never accept your authority. Besides, legally, I would think now this man has leased it, it's his land for as long as the lease states.'

'But Dad doesn't know anything—if he did he'd have told me. Come on, Keanu, you must know something.'

'All I know is that some rich man is turning it into a resort. A chap called Luke Wilson was doing some research here a few years ago and apparently this rich bloke knew Luke from somewhere. That was enough for Ian to make contact with him and that's what happened.'

Keanu paused, trying to think—to get it right.

'I wouldn't be surprised if he's already achieved his aim for the resort—there's been a hell of a lot of activity going on around the place. Container loads of stuff taken off huge ships and ferried ashore on barges, imported workers everywhere.'

'But the research station? That was my great-grandfather's legacy to the whole of M'Langi, designed to provide facilities and housing to anyone who wanted to investigate or study ways to improve the health of the islanders through science. Your father was one of the first to work there. I know my grandfather and Ian resented putting money into it, but I'm sure it was legally tied up so the mine had to keep supporting it.'

'And if the mine couldn't?' Keanu asked. 'Isn't it better to lease it to someone with money than let the idea die completely?'

Caroline stared at him, trying to work out what might be going on behind this conversation.

As far as she was concerned, there was a lot of very strange stuff lingering in the deep recesses of her mind and fluttering along the nerves in her body, yet Keanu was sitting there, about as sensitive as a boulder.

Whatever. She was finding out things she needed to know so she had to set aside all the physical manifestations of the boulder's presence and seek more information.

'You mean this mystery millionaire is going to keep the research station going? So why build luxury accommodation?'

Keanu shrugged.

'Who knows, but that's what's happening because Sam's been carrying on with some of Luke's research into why the islanders don't suffer from encephalitis to the extent their counterparts in other island groups do and he's been wanting to use the laboratories there. Apparently, they've said he can as soon as the renovations are completed.'

'Weirder and weirder,' Caroline muttered, but the worst of the weirdness was what was going on in her body. She'd been, what, thirteen when she'd last seen Keanu? And with her isolated life on the island then boarding school, had probably been a late developer. And although his disappearance from her life had devastated her—even broken her heart—it had been a child's heart that had been broken, a child's love betrayed.

What she was feeling now had nothing childish about it, and if she was going to be working with him, seeing him every day, she'd better get over whatever it was PDQ.

Practicalities—they would be the best antidote to this Keanu business.

'Let's go and see,' she suggested. 'I'll grab some bottled water and a torch, and we'll go take a look.'

'We can't,' Keanu answered flatly, killing the small spark of excitement taking some action had lit.

'And why not?' she demanded, the young Caroline again.

'I've already told you, it's fenced off. Visitors to the resort won't be bumped along a rocky track—they'll travel down there by helicopter.'

'They can't have fenced the whole place. Not the beach and the reef and that rockfall around the corner of Sunset Beach.'

'So?'

'We'll just have to find our way either around or over this fence and see what's happening for ourselves. We'll go down to the beach for a start, and walk to the rockfall then figure it out from there. We've swum around it in the past, but it might be low tide. We should at least go and have a look.'

She was twelve again and grinned at him.

'Come on, Keanu, it will be an adventure, just like old times!'

Keanu studied the beautiful, *smiling* woman in front of him and knew that while her features might have changed as she'd matured, her determination obviously had not.

He heard his mother's voice, back when they'd been young, saying look after Caroline—words to a child that were now coming back to haunt him. He'd *have* to go along on this ridiculous escapade because there was no way he could let her go alone. The very thought of her prowling around down there made his blood run cold, not to mention what might happen if she tried to climb the rockfall on her own.

Apart from which, he had to admit, he *would* like to know what was going on at the northern end of the island, and he could check out if they'd rebuilt the longhouse and if it would be suitable for Alkiri's funeral feast—should they get permission to use it.

'Are you going like that?' he asked, looking at the short shift dress she wore.

'Of course,' she replied. 'It's faded so much it almost

looks like camouflage, although I didn't choose it for that—just pulled it out of the cupboard. I'll slip on some soft dive boots in case we have to swim.'

He hoped like hell they wouldn't have to swim, because the thought of seeing that shift wet and clinging to her body was already causing a definite stirring in his lower abdomen.

The thought of helping her down the cliff path, taking her elbow on a tricky bit, touching her at all, had been bad enough, but the wet shift image was torturous.

Yet he'd seen Caroline naked often enough, when they'd shucked off their clothes to swim in the lagoon by the house—but that had been boy-girl stuff, kid stuff—and she hadn't had breasts then...

Dear heaven, was he losing his mind?

He knew his mother had had good reason for leaving the island—Ian Lockhart had made sure of that—but he wondered if she'd also been thinking of what might happen as he and Caroline went through puberty? Feeling as she did about Ian, his having a relationship with Ian's niece might have been too much...

Caroline was back, soft dive boots—more like ballet slippers—on her feet and a small backpack on her back. She passed a second one to him.

'A camera with a long-distance lens,' she announced. 'Apparently, Ian didn't know of Dad's interest in photography or he'd have found them and sold them off as he seems to have done with everything else of value in the house.'

Keanu thought of the beautiful pieces of porcelain Caro's grandmother had collected—and Caro had loved—and knew without asking that they'd be gone.

Well, he hadn't been able to save her treasures, but he sure as hell was going to do everything he could to keep her safe in her mad quest to save the island. At least in *that* quest they'd be partners once again.

He slung the backpack over his shoulder and reached out to take her arm.

'Let's go,' he said. She moved away from his outstretched hand, but undeterred he added, 'It *will* be like old times!'

Except all his senses were on full alert, his body buzzing just being near her, so who the hell knew what would happen if she actually swam!

CHAPTER FOUR

THEY WALKED SWIFTLY to the clifftop, muscle memory in their feet remembering the path possibly better than their brains did. Above them, in the thick rainforest, birds were settling down for the night, rustling among the leaves. Then down the rocky track with its views out over the reef to the ocean beyond. The path they took was now overgrown in places as if it had been rarely used since two adventurous children had left the island.

'How long have you been here?'

Caroline, following him with one hand on his backpack, asked the question.

'Three weeks.'

The answer came easily. Three weeks of shock as he'd tried to accept the island as it was now and work out what had happened.

'Have you seen the Blakes?'

Keanu shook his head.

'They were long gone when I got here. The old man, your grandfather, appointed Peter not long before he died and your father was happy to leave him in charge of the mine when you were born and he had to take Christopher to the mainland for constant medical supervision.'

'Dad liked the fact that Peter was an engineer as well

as having practical knowledge as a miner, and he was as honest as they come.'

'Probably too honest for Ian,' Keanu said. 'He decided he could do the job better and sacked Peter. Then, with Peter gone, Ian announced he'd take over the running of the mine as well as everything else on the island.'

'No wonder it's run-down,' Caro said tartly. 'Ian couldn't manage his way out of an open door.'

'Harsh!' Keanu said, turning to take Caro's hand and help her over a particularly tricky bit of the path.

'Well, you know he couldn't. The only things he was ever interested in were money and women and gambling, although I imagine the order changed according to the situation.'

And even in the dim light of early evening reflected off the sea she saw the pain on Keanu's face, the stricken look in his eyes. She remembered something strange that Bessie had said about it being better if Kari kept her distance from Ian, and started to connect the dots…

'Oh, Keanu, not your mother?' She reached for his shoulders and pulled him close, wrapping her arms awkwardly around his body. 'Is that why you left? Why didn't she tell my father? Or the elders? Or the police? Do something to get him stopped?'

Keanu eased out of her grasp and looked down at her, his face now wiped as blank as she'd ever seen it.

'He didn't assault her, if that's what you're thinking,' he said. 'What he did was worse.'

Bitterness as harsh and hurtful as Caroline had ever heard leached from every word so each one was a separate prick of pain—into her skin, through her flesh and into her heart.

But worse than rape?

What could she say?

Much as she longed to know more, she knew by the cold finality in Keanu's voice that the conversation was finished.

He had turned and was moving on and although she longed to ask him if that's why he'd never contacted her, she knew she wouldn't—couldn't. In fact, she knew the answer.

Somehow or other, a Lockhart had hurt his mother—an unforgiveable sin.

They stumbled their way down to the beach then, staying in the shadows of the fringing coconut palms, made their way to the rockfall.

The tide was in, the small ripples of water inside the reef splashing up against the rocks.

'So we swim,' she said brightly, wishing they could get back to the not easy, but easier atmosphere they'd shared as they'd started down the cliff. 'But I doubt Dad's camera's waterproof so what if I go around first then climb up on the lower rocks on the other side and you pass it to me, then you swim around?'

'Haven't changed much, have you? Bossy as ever!' Keanu muttered, and Caroline hid a smile—the old Keanu was back with her again, if only temporarily.

It was far worse than he'd expected, Keanu realised as Caro, the thin wet shift clinging to every curve of her body, appeared on the other side of the rockfall, reaching up and out for the rucksack.

He'd taken off his shirt but his shorts would be wet as he clambered ashore, so his reaction would be obvious, though it was darker now and maybe she wouldn't notice…

Well, he could hardly leave her alone on the other side of the rockfall—not with his mother's order, the 'take care of Caroline' one, still echoing in his ears.

He swam, emerging from the lagoon and flapping at his shorts to conceal the evidence of his reaction.

'We'd better move into the shadows of the palm trees,'

he said, deciding it was time to take charge. 'And walk quietly. You don't know who might be around.'

'What, like fierce Alsatian guard dogs that will rip us
to pieces without a second thought?' Caroline muttered. 'I
wonder if I can still shin up a coconut palm.'

Keanu smiled at the image, although he was thinking
more of the darkness the shadows would provide. At least
in the shadows beneath the palms he wouldn't be able to see
the way her full breasts were outlined by the wet shift, or
the way it was indented into her navel, and raised slightly
over the mound of her sex.

He had to stop thinking about wet shifts and sex and
concentrate or they'd be caught for sure.

As they approached the first of the bures that had once
housed visiting scientists they heard voices, but not close.

'That sounds like people over beyond the kitchen where
the little staff bar used to be,' he murmured to Caroline.

The helicopter pilots, back when there had been three or
four and so they'd had more time off than other staff, had
always frequented it, not by creeping down the cliff and
swimming around the rockfall but by walking down the
track from the airfield—the track now fenced off, guarded
and gated.

A lone light shone in the first of the bures, but even from
outside Keanu could see the place had had a lot of money
spent on it. Stone walls where mud had been, a marble deck
with a deep spa bath shaded by thick vegetation.

'This isn't accommodation for visiting scientists,' Caro
whispered to him. 'It's luxury accommodation for the very
wealthy who want absolute privacy and can afford it. See
how each bure has been separated from the next by a thick
planting of shrubs, most of them scented, like that huge
ginger plant over there.'

'But what of the laboratories and the communal kitchens and dining rooms?' he argued. 'Surely people paying

the kind of money they'd pay to stay here aren't all going to eat together?

'Let's see.'

Keanu took her hand, ignoring the shock of excitement such an impersonal touch had caused. He led the way towards the kitchen area, although always off the path that, even in the dark, looked freshly raked and would show their footprints.

What had been the kitchen and adjoining open eating area seemed shrouded in scaffolding, until they crept closer and realised the old longhouse had been included in the renovations. It was now a longer, wider building, still open at the sides to catch the breezes, exactly like the meeting halls on the other islands, where feasts were held and elders met to make rules or administer judgment. Only better—fancier…

The kitchens must be behind it, but so was the bar because the noise was louder now.

'We can't go farther,' Keanu said firmly. 'We'd be caught for sure. We'll have to rely on Sam to report on the laboratories when he's able to go back to work in them. And there's no way we can take photographs, the flash would alert someone for sure.'

He half expected Caro to argue—she'd always been the one more willing to take risks—but to his surprise she turned back into the bushes.

'Come on, we'll go back the way we came before someone finds us.'

Caroline smiled to herself, realising Keanu was now as intent on this expedition as she had been.

But holding Keanu's hand was distracting, and he was pulling her along, far too close to his body, which was beyond distracting. She began to tremble and suspected it wasn't nerves or cold, although he stopped in a particular dense patch of shadow and pulled her into his arms.

'You're cold,' he whispered, folding her against his body, the action making her tremble even more. His bare skin was warm against hers, his body hard where hers was soft. And her reaction to it was so startling she probably would have done something stupid like kiss him if he hadn't been rubbing his hands up and down her arms, obviously trying to warm her, although the trembles had nothing to do with the cool night air.

A boulder—it confirmed her suspicions. No matter what weird reactions she was having to this reunion—to his closeness, his body—he was feeling nothing for the woman trembling in his arms.

A rustle in the bushes broke them apart, and although it was only an inquisitive lyrebird, it was enough to remind them of where they were and the inherent danger of being caught there.

But red flags of warning of another kind waved in Caroline's head as they crept back to the beach. Her reaction to Keanu holding her had to be a rebound thing. Devastated by Steve's rejection and reunited with her childhood friend, she'd really only wanted comfort.

Right.

So why was her body throbbing with what felt very like desire, not to mention an even deeper regret that the kiss hadn't happened?

Ridiculous! A relationship between them just couldn't happen. Not only had her uncle Ian done all he could to blacken the Lockhart name among the islands' population but he'd—what?—assaulted Keanu's mother?

Although he'd said worse than assault…

Little wonder Keanu had broken off all contact with her—and probably distrusted anyone who bore the Lockhart name.

At which stage she fell over, making enough noise as she landed in a baby palm tree to awaken the ghosts of the dead.

'What is wrong with you?' Keanu growled, hauling her to her feet. 'You're blundering along as if you've got your eyes shut.'

She could hardly tell him the line her thoughts had been following so she got back onto the edge of the path and resumed walking quietly along it.

'Tomorrow night we could walk along the fence,' Keanu said, breaking a silence that had stretched a little tautly between them.

'I might be on duty. I haven't met Hettie yet, let alone get a roster from her.'

'Come to think of it, you probably will be on duty,' Keanu told her. 'Anahera does extra day shifts so she can be at home with Hana in the evenings. Besides which we probably wouldn't see much—the plantings are too thick.'

'On duty all night?' Caroline ignored his fence conversation because she was interested in the set-up at the short-staffed hospital, although she'd get back to him ordering her around some other time. They'd been a pair, a partnership, in all the right and wrong things they'd done, and now here he was, giving orders...

'No, three to midnight. We have a couple of local nurses' aides who share the night shifts between them.'

'And who supports them?'

Keanu sighed.

'It's a small hospital, Caro, and either Sam or whatever doctor is here is always on call. Hettie, too, for that matter. The staff quarters are just at the back of the hospital and it takes exactly two minutes to get from one of our apartments to the wards.'

'You've timed it?'

They'd reached the beach and paused beneath the palm

trees, talking quietly while they checked that no one else was taking a midnight stroll.

'I've done it,' Keanu told her. 'More than once. The aides are good, but they know what they can handle and what they can't. The system could be a lot better but it works.'

It didn't seem right to Caroline that Hettie was the nurse always on call, but until she knew more about the hospital, there was nothing she could do.

She was concentrating on hospital staffing issues because Keanu's use of her childhood name—his casual use of 'Caro'—had started up the disturbances the warming hug had caused.

'It seems quiet, let's go,' she said, and led the way across the sand to the shadow of the rockfall.

To Keanu's relief the tide had gone out far enough for them to wade around the rocks. Given the effect that holding her had had on his body, he didn't think he could handle seeing the wet shift again.

He had no idea why Caro had returned to the island, certain her coming to help because she'd heard it was in trouble wasn't the whole story.

What had happened to that sleazy-looking guy called Steve who was always with her in the society pictures?

Had he dumped her?

Keanu shook his head, angry with himself for even thinking about Caroline's private life, but angrier for feeling sorry for her. It was bad enough he'd become involved in tonight's escapade, but to have held Caro in his arms, felt her body pressed to his...

He must have been moonstruck!

They were scaling the rocky cliff path now and he paused to look around for a moon but failed to find one.

'Are you grunting?' Caro asked. 'I know it's steep but I thought you'd be fitter than that.'

'I was *not* grunting,' he told her, voice as cold as he could make it.

'Wild pigs, then,' Carol said cheerfully, although he knew she didn't for a minute believe it.

Though would she have believed he'd been grunting at his own stupid thoughts?

'Bright lights ahead,' the woman he shouldn't have held in his arms said cheerfully, and he locked away the past and moved himself swiftly into the present.

Bright lights indeed.

'The helicopter must have brought in a patient from an outer island,' he said, lengthening his stride so he passed Caro as he hurried towards the scene of the action.

Hettie had one end of the stretcher they were unloading, Jack, the pilot, holding the other end. He could see Manu, their one remaining hospital orderly, running towards the airstrip, Sam not far behind him.

'Tropical ulcer gone bad,' Hettie said as Manu took over her end of the stretcher and Sam and Keanu arrived. 'I'm actually dubious about it. I think it might be worse than that.'

'A Buruli ulcer?' Sam queried, and Hettie shrugged.

'We'll need to test it.'

She spoke quietly but Keanu knew they were all feeling tension from the words she'd spoken. Tropical ulcers were common enough and in many cases very difficult to treat, but the Buruli was a whole other species, and could lead to bone involvement and permanent disability.

'Is it common here?'

He'd forgotten about Caro but she was right behind him, so close that when he swung around to answer her his arm brushed against her breast.

And restarted all the thoughts he was sure he'd locked away.

'Not as common as in some islands in the west Pacific,'

he told her, then he caught up with Hettie, who was following the stretcher up the slight incline to the hospital.

'I've got a new recruit for you here,' he said. 'Sam's probably told you Maddie and the FIFO nurse weren't coming in today, but Caroline dropped from the skies yesterday and she tells us she's a nurse.'

He ignored the glower Caro shot at him as she stepped past him to introduce herself to Hettie.

'Caroline Lockhart,' she said, holding out her hand, while Keanu watched the meeting with some trepidation.

'Of the hilltop mansion Lockharts?' Hettie demanded, ignoring the proffered hand.

'Yes, and proud of it,' Caro said quietly but firmly. 'And I'd rather be judged by my work than the house I live in.'

Hettie pushed errant bits of hair off her forehead and sighed.

'Fair call,' she said softly, and this time, to Keanu's relief, *she* held out *her* hand. 'It's just been too long a day trying to work out how to replace a resident clinic nurse on Raiki Island.'

'What happened to her?' Caroline asked, and Keanu knew the answer was going to hurt her.

'Apparently she went off with your uncle Ian—she and all the drugs.'

'She what?' Caroline swung towards Keanu. 'Does my father know all that's been going on? Know his brother's stooped so low as to rob an island of their drugs, not to mention their nurse?'

'It was only discovered yesterday.' Hettie answered for him, and her voice was gentle. 'And as Ian's gone off in his yacht to who knows where, there's very little your father or anyone else can do about it.'

Keanu read the pain on Caro's face as she realised exactly why the Lockhart name was mud. The harm Ian had done reached out across all island life and all the islanders.

Following the little procession up to the hospital, Keanu felt deeply sorry for her, sorry for the pain the slights against her family must be causing her.

But the Caro he'd known would have pushed away any offer of comfort and tossed her head to deny any pain.

He glanced towards her and saw her chin rise.

This Caro wasn't so different. She'd take them all on and prove all Lockharts weren't tarred with the same brush.

And seeing that chin tilt—reading it—his heart cramped just a little at the sight of it. The woman she'd become wasn't so different from his Caro after all.

'A Buruli ulcer?'

Caroline had caught up with him so the question came from his right shoulder.

He glanced towards her and even in the poor light on the track he could see the remnants of her hurt.

He wanted to put his arm around her shoulders and pull her close. Comfort her as he had when she'd been a child, hurt or lonely or bewildered by her motherless, and usually fatherless, situation.

But with all the new disturbances she'd caused in his body, giving her a comforting hug was no longer an option.

Professional colleagues, that's all they were.

'It's not that common but it's a nasty thing if left untended, as this one may have been. Often it starts as a small nodule, hardly bigger than a mosquito bite, so the patient just ignores it, but the infection can lead to a bigger ulcer forming, destroying skin and tissue. If it's left too long there can be bone involvement, even loss of a limb.'

'Sounds like a similar infection to leprosy.' She was frowning now, no doubt thinking back to her years of study.

'Spot on,' he told her. 'The bacterium causing it is related to both the leprosy and tuberculosis bacteria.'

'Can you test for it here or do you have to send swabs to the mainland? Wouldn't that take days?'

Hettie answered for him.

'We're fortunate in that Sam is an avid bacteriologist in whatever spare time he has. Although the research station's closed at the moment, he still loves poking around in the little lab we have at the hospital and breeding who knows what in Petri dishes. If anyone can test it, he can.'

Caroline realised she'd have to rethink the laid-back, handsome doctor who ran the hospital. He obviously had hidden depths because even the simplest of biological tests was painstaking work.

They'd reached the hospital and, unsure of her part in whatever lay ahead, she followed the troop inside.

The patient was young, maybe just reaching teenage years, from French Island, so called, Caroline knew, because a French square-rigged sailing vessel had once foundered there, the sailors staying on, intermarrying with the locals, until rescued many years later.

Caroline concentrated on the now instead of on the past. The boy, Raoul—French names still being common—had been lifted onto an examination table, and Sam, assisted by one of the nurses' aides who had been waiting at the hospital, was carefully removing the light dressing Hettie had used to cover the wound.

Caroline swallowed a gasp. This was no small nodule like a mosquito bite but a full-blown leg ulcer, the edges a mess of tattered skin and deeper down, tender, infected flesh.

'I'm going to take a swab,' Sam was saying to the patient, 'but even before I test it, I'm going to start you on antibiotics.'

'It generally responds well to a combination of rifampicin and streptomycin,' Keanu explained quietly. 'If that doesn't work, there are other combinations of drugs we can use, usually with the rifampicin. The other combinations haven't been fully tested but the options are there.'

Tension she hadn't been aware she was feeling eased a little, but she hated the thought of the possibility of this young lad losing a leg.

'Okay, everyone out except Mina,' Sam said, using a shooing motion with his hand. 'She and I can handle it from here. Keanu, you might introduce our newest staff member to Jack. And Hettie, if you're not too tired, I've left Caroline's details on your desk, but you might want a chat with her yourself.'

Great, Caroline thought. A perfect end to a perfect day—an interview with a woman who obviously hated her entire family.

But Keanu had taken her elbow, and all thoughts but her reactions to his closeness fled from her mind.

'Come out and meet Jack Richards,' he said. 'There's a staffroom through here—we can have a coffee or a cold drink.'

A bit social for an introduction, Caroline thought, but apparently the pilot called Jack usually made for this staffroom when he returned from a flight. And, yes, he was sitting there, legs outstretched on a tilting lounge chair, draining the last dregs from a can of cola.

With his head tilted back, she could see a jutting jaw, and the breadth of his shoulders suggested muscle rather than fat. Here, in the light, she saw he was tall, but solid rather than rangy. His dark hair was cropped close to his scalp as if he ran an electric razor over it every now and then by way of hairdressing.

He had a strong face, a slightly skewed nose that suggested football in his youth, and smooth olive skin. But by far his most arresting feature was a pair of dark blue eyes, which, Caroline guessed, missed very little.

He set the empty can down on a small side table.

'God, I needed that,' he said. 'The day was a disaster from beginning to end. First the consequences of the disappearance of the drugs and the nurse from Raiki. You can imagine how angry the residents were. Then we headed over to Atangi because there are two nurses there and Hettie hoped one of them would cover Raiki until we got someone.'

'Did you get someone?' Caroline asked, intrigued by this idea of a helicopter flitting between the islands as casually as a city commute.

'Yes, I think so. Hett's still negotiating. Anyway, who do we find but a mum who'd mistaken clinic days and brought in a toddler for vaccination? A toddler who hated needles. Poor kid, who doesn't? He screamed like a banshee as Hettie gave him his triple antigen. Of course, the father came in and got stuck into Hettie and the scene developed into something like an old-time TV comedy, only it wasn't really funny because the poor kid was genuinely terrified.'

'Then French and the ulcer,' Keanu said, turning from the urn where he'd been making a coffee—holding out the cup to Caroline, who shook her head.

'Yeah, we had a call from the nurse there, whipped over and collected the lad, then to top it all off we were caught in a very nasty crosswind on the flight home. I know we have to expect that at this time of the year—it's the start of cyclone season—but heaven help us if there's an emergency call tonight.'

'You're the only pilot?' Caroline asked, sitting down on the couch across from Jack.

'Sorry, I'm supposed to make the introductions,' Keanu said. 'Jack, this is Caroline, new nurse. Caroline, this is Jack Richards and, yes, at the moment he's our only pilot. Although there's relief on the way Friday when the second flight for the week comes in. That's right, isn't it, Jack? A FIFO coming in to give you a break?'

'Yeah, young Matt Rogers is due to come in on Friday's flight.'

'You don't like him?' Caroline asked, unable to not hear the distaste in Jack's voice.

'Only because he's younger, and fitter and better looking than our Jack here,' Keanu teased, 'and they both share a very keen interest in the beautiful Anahera.'

'Who at least ignores us both equally,' Jack said with such gloom Caroline had to smile.

'I can't blame any man being attracted to her—she *is* beautiful,' Caroline said, now wondering if the nurse was ignoring these two suitors because she had her eye on someone else.

Someone like Keanu?

And if Vailea's daughter fancied Keanu and Vailea was thinking him a good match, maybe that's why she'd shown such animosity to Caroline. Everyone on the island would know the two of them had grown up together...

She must have sighed, for Keanu said, 'Come on, you're tired. I'll walk you up to the house.'

Jack straightened up in his chair.

'*The* house?' he said. 'Like the Lockhart mansion? Since when did our nurses get lucky enough to stay there while important blokes like me sleep in little better than prefabricated huts?'

'Since their surname is Lockhart,' Keanu said, enough ice in his voice to stop further speculation. 'And *all* the hospital buildings are prefabricated, as you well know. It makes it much easier to pack them into shipping containers and land them here, then it only needs a small team of men to put them together.'

He turned to Caroline.

'Prefab or not, the staff villas are really lovely so just ignore him.'

Jack was ignoring them both. He was still staring at Caroline.

'You're a Lockhart?' he said with such disbelief Caroline had to smile.

'Did you think we all had two heads?' she asked, but Jack continued to stare at her.

Maybe she *had* grown a second head.

But two heads would give her two brains and she only needed one—even a part of one—to know she didn't want Keanu walking her home. Her feelings towards him were in such turmoil she doubted she'd ever sort them out.

For years she'd hated him for his desertion. Hadn't he realised he'd been her only true friend? Even after they'd both gone to boarding school, he'd still been the person to whom she'd poured out her heart in letter after letter.

Her homesickness, the strange emptiness that came from being motherless, the pain of her time spent with Christopher, who couldn't respond to her words of love—writing to Keanu had been a way of getting it out of her system.

So he knew everything there was to know about her life, from her envy when other girls' parents came to special occasions to the realisation that, for her father, Christopher and the hospital on Wildfire were more important than she was.

She'd told Keanu things she'd never told anyone, before or since, then suddenly, he'd been gone.

Nothing.

Until now, and although the confusion of seeing him again had at first been confined to her head, since he'd held her—if only to warm her—it was in her heart as well.

Damn the man.

'I don't need you to walk me home,' she said when they'd left the staffroom. 'I *do* know the way.'

'And *I* know there are a lot of unhappy Lockhart employees—or ex-employees—on the island at the moment, and while I don't think for a minute they'd take out their frustration on you, I'd rather be sure than sorry.'

So he was walking her home to protect her. Looking after Caroline as his mother had always told him to when they'd been children.

She felt stupidly disappointed at this realisation then told herself she was just being ridiculous.

As if that kind of a hug meant anything. And anyway she didn't want Keanu hugging her.

That just added to her torment.

'What employees and ex-employees are upset?' she asked to take her mind off things she couldn't handle right now.

'Just about all of them,' Keanu replied. 'But mostly the miners, and although some of them are from other islands, a lot of them live in the village. They've had their hours cut and the ones who've been sacked haven't been paid back wages, let alone their superannuation.'

'But if Ian's gone, who's here to pay them or to cut hours? Who's running the mine?'

'Who knows? Ian's disappearance, as you may have gathered, is fairly recent. He was here last week, then suddenly he was either holed up in the house or gone.'

'Gone how?' Caroline asked as they reached the front steps of the house, where Bessie had left a welcoming light burning.

'Presumably on his yacht. It was a tidy size. One day it was in the mine harbour and the next it was gone.'

'But the mine's still operating?'

Keanu nodded.

'Then we should go down and check it out.'

'Go down to the mine?' Keanu demanded.

Caroline grinned at him.

'Not right now, you goose, but tomorrow or whenever we can get some time off together. That's if you want to come with me.'

'Well, I damn well wouldn't let you go alone, although why you want to go—'

'Because I need to know—*we* need to know. Without the mine there's no way we can keep the hospital going, not to mention the fact that the entire population, not just those here on Wildfire, will lose their medical facilities as well as their incomes.'

She was so excited her eyes gleamed in the moonlight, and it was all Keanu could to not take her in his arms again, only this time for a different reason.

But if holding her once had been a mistake, twice would be fatal.

And he was still married—or probably still married, even if he hadn't seen his wife for five years.

Did that matter?

Of course it did.

He could hardly start something that she might think would lead to marriage if he couldn't marry her.

So forget a hug.

'We can't run the mine,' he said, far too bluntly because now a different confusion was nagging at him.

She shook her head in irritation.

'Then we'll just have to think of something.'

He had to agree, if only silently. The continued survival of the hospital—in fact, of all the health care in the islands—depended on support from the mine.

'I imagine once we know what's happening we can find someone who can,' he said, reluctantly drawn in and now thinking aloud. 'Some of the local men have worked there since it opened, or if they're not still there we could find them. We want men who trained under Peter Blake or maybe beg Peter to come back.'

'And pay him how?' Caroline demanded.

Keanu held up his hands in surrender.

'Hey, you're the one who wanted to think of something. I'm just throwing out ideas here. You can take them or leave them.'

He saw the shadow cross her face and knew he'd somehow said the wrong thing.

'Is that how you felt about me back then? That you could take me or leave me? Yes, Ian obviously hurt your mother, but what did *I* do to *you* to make you cut me out of your life?'

She was angry—beautiful with anger—but he stood his ground, then he leaned forward and touched her very gently on the cheek.

'You were never right out of my life, Caro,' he said quietly, his hand sliding down to rest on her shoulder. Momentarily. He turned and walked swiftly back down the track, not wanting her to see the pain her words had caused written clearly on his face.

But she was right. He *had* come back to see what he could do to save the hospital, and saving the mine should have been the obvious starting place.

But joining forces in this crusade would mean seeing more of her, working with her outside hospital hours, feeling her body beside his, aware all the time of the effect she had on him, aware of her in a way he'd never been before, or imagined he ever would.

Physically aware of the one woman in the world who was beyond his grasp—the woman whose trust he'd betrayed when she'd been nothing more than a girl...

Caroline watched him stride down the path, long legs moving smoothly and deliberately over the rough track, stance upright, broad shoulders square...

Was it just the length of time since they'd seen each

other that was making things so awkward between them, or was Keanu still brooding over whatever had happened to make him stop writing to her? Even stop reading her letters…

'Bother the man,' she muttered to herself, climbing the steps and wandering through the house towards her bedroom.

Her bedroom. Still decorated with the posters of the idols of her teenage self.

Of course, with Ian gone, she could have the pick of any of the six bedrooms in the house, but her room felt like home, even if home was an empty and lonely place without Keanu in it. Helen *and* Keanu. Their rooms had been in the western annexe, but the whole house had been her and Keanu's playground—the whole island, in fact.

Stupid tears pricked behind her eyelids as memories of their youth together—their friendship and closeness—threatened to overwhelm her.

Pulling herself together, she ripped the posters off the walls. One day soon—when she'd done the things she *really* needed to do, like visit the mine, she'd find some paint and redo the room, maybe redecorate the whole house, removing all traces of the past.

Except in your head, a traitorous voice reminded her.

But she'd had enough of traitorous voices—hadn't one lived with her through most of her relationship with Steve?

She'd learned to ignore it and could do so again.

Although, with Steve, maybe she'd have been better off listening to it. Listening to the whisper that had questioned his protestations of love, listened to the niggling murmur that had questioned broken dates with facile excuses, listened to her friends…

Had she been so desperate for love, for someone to love her, that she'd ignored all the signs and warnings?

'Oh, for heaven's sake, get with it, girl!' she said out loud, hoping to jolt herself from the past to the present.

There was certainly enough to be done in the present to blot out any voices in her head.

Work was the answer. Nursing at the hospital, and during her time off finding out exactly what had been happening on the island.

CHAPTER FIVE

THE PREVIOUS EVENING Hettie had disappeared by the time Caroline had finished talking to Jack, so she wasn't sure if she was employed or not. Deciding she had to find out, she walked down to the hospital at seven-thirty the next morning.

It was already hot and the humidity was rising. Jack's mention of cyclones had reminded her that this wasn't the best time of the year to return to the island—although she'd spent many long summer holidays here and survived whatever the weather had thrown at her.

Hettie was in a side ward with the patient she'd brought in the previous evening, and it was, Caroline decided, almost inevitable that Keanu would be with her as she examined the wound.

'Will you have to cut away the ulcerated tissue?' she asked, walking to the other side of the bed and peering at the ulcer herself.

Hettie looked up, beautiful green eyes focussing on Caroline.

Focussing so intently Caroline found herself offering a shrug that wasn't exactly an apology for speaking but very nearly.

'I came down to see if you had work for me to do—a slot in the roster perhaps, or some use you could put me to?'

Hettie was still eyeing her warily, or maybe that was just her everyday look. She was neat—a slim figure, jeans and a white shirt, long dark hair controlled in a perfect roll at the back of her head—and attractive in a way that made Caroline think she'd be beautiful if she smiled.

'What do you know about Buruli ulcers?' Hettie asked, and, breathing silent thanks for the instinct that had made her look them up on the internet, Caroline rattled off what she'd learned.

Then, aware that the internet wasn't always right, she added, 'But that's just what Mr Google told me. I haven't had any experience of them.'

To her surprise, Hettie smiled and Caroline saw that she *was* beautiful—that quiet, unexpected kind of beauty that was rare enough to sometimes go unnoticed.

'You'll do,' Hettie said. 'Welcome aboard. It's hard to work to rosters here, but there's always work. Maddie, one of our FIFO doctors, usually does the checks on the miners but she didn't come in and the checks are due—or slightly overdue. You'd know the mine, wouldn't you? Perhaps you and Keanu could do that today?'

Excitement fizzed in Caroline's head—the perfect excuse to go down to the mine.

'What kind of checks do we do?' she asked Hettie, ignoring Keanu, who was arguing that she was too new in the job to be going down to the mine.

'Just general health. They tend to ignore cuts and scratches, although they know they can become infected or even ulcerated. And we've got a couple of workers—you'll see their notes on the cards—who we suspect have chest problems and aren't really suited to working underground. But you know men, they're a stubborn lot and will argue until they're blue in the face that they haven't any problems with their lungs.'

'Stubborn patients I do understand,' Carolyn said, smiling inwardly as she wondered if seemingly prim and proper Hettie had experienced many run-ins with stubborn men in her own life. She certainly seemed to have some strong opinions when it came to men in general.

'As a matter of course,' Hettie continued, 'we check the lung capacity of all the men and keep notes, and those two aren't so bad we can order them out of the mine. Yet. The hospital is, in part, funded by the Australian government, and the health checks at the mine are a Workplace Health and Safety requirement.'

'More paperwork for Sam,' Caroline said, and Hettie smiled again.

'He does hate it,' she agreed before turning to Keanu. 'You're not tied up, so you can take Caroline down there. You can show her where all the paperwork is kept, and the drugs cabinet we have down there.'

'If Ian didn't pinch it when he left,' Keanu muttered, but Caroline couldn't help feeling how lucky they were, to both have this excuse to visit the mine.

And although more time with Keanu was hardly ideal, this was work, and all she had to do was concentrate on that.

If she was gathering whatever impressions she could of what was happening at the mine she'd hardly be aware Keanu was there.

Hardly.

Stick to business!

'So, who do you think will be in charge of the mine now Ian's gone?' she asked Keanu as they took the path around the house that led to the steps down to the mine.

He stopped, turning around to take her hand to help her over a rough part of the track where the stone steps had broken away.

'Ian's never really been hands-on, leaving the shift bosses to run the teams. Reuben Alaki is one of the best,' he said, speaking so calmly she knew he couldn't possibly be feeling all the physical reactions to the touch that were surging through her.

'I remember Reuben,' she managed to say, hoping she sounded as calm as he had, although she was certain there'd been a quiver in her voice. 'His wife died and he had to bring his little boy to work and your mother looked after him. We treated him like a pet dog or cat and he followed us everywhere.'

Fortunately for her sanity the rough bit of track was behind them, and Keanu had released her hand.

'That's him, although that little boy is grown up and is over in Australia, getting paid obscene amounts of money to play football.'

Then of course Keanu smiled, which had much the same result on her nerve endings as his touch had.

'Good for him,' Caroline said cheerily. 'Maybe you should have gone that way instead of becoming a doctor.'

Then you wouldn't be here holding my hand and smiling at me and totally confusing me!

Lost in her own thoughts, she didn't realise Keanu had stopped. He turned back to face her, his face taut with emotion.

'We had an agreement,' he reminded her, and now a sudden sadness—nostalgia for their carefree past, their happy childhood—swept over her.

'What happened to us, Keanu?' she whispered, forgetting the present, remembering only the past.

'Ian happened,' he said bluntly, and continued down the path.

Guilt kept him moving, because he *could* have kept in touch with Caroline, but in his anger—an impotent rage at his mother's pain—he had himself cursed all Lockharts.

Of course it had had nothing to do with Caroline, but

at the time fury had made him blind and deaf, then, with his mother's death, it had been all he could do just to keep going. Getting back in touch with Caroline had been the last thing on his mind.

'All the files are in the site office,' he said, all business now as they reached the bottom of the steps.

He pointed to the rusty-looking shed sheltering under the overhang of the cave that led into the mine.

'That's Reuben there now. Let's go and see him.'

He knew Caroline was close behind him, aware of her in every fibre of his body, yet his mind was crowded with practical matters and he needed to concentrate on them—on the now, not the past...

The rumbling noise from deep inside the tunnel told him the mine was still being worked, but who was paying the men? And the crushing plant and extraction machine were standing idle, so they could hardly be taking home their wages in gold.

'Who's paying the men?' Caroline asked, as if she'd been following his train of thought as well as his footsteps.

'Reuben will tell us.'

Reuben stepped out of the shed to shake Keanu's hand, then turned to Caroline.

'New nurse?' he asked.

'But old friend, I hope, Reuben. It's Caroline Lockhart.'

Reuben beamed with delight and held out his arms to give Caroline a hug.

'You've grown up!' Reuben said, looking fondly at her. 'Grown up and beautiful!'

And from the look on Caroline's face, it was the first friendly greeting she'd received since her return.

'And your father? How is he?' Reuben asked.

'Working too hard. I hardly see him.'

'Working and caring for that poor brother of yours, too, I suppose. Same as always,' Reuben said. 'Me, I did that when my wife died but later I realised pain didn't go away with work. I have a new wife now and new family, and my big boy, he's rich and famous in Australia—sends money home to his old man even.'

'That's great, Reuben,' Caroline said, and Keanu knew she meant it. Her affinity for the islanders had always been as strong as his, and they had known that and loved her for it.

'So, what's happening here, Reuben?' he asked to get his mind back on track.

'Well…'

Reuben paused, scratched his head, shuffled his feet, and finally waved them both inside.

'The men working the bulldozer and crusher and extraction plant hadn't been paid for more than a month so they walked off the job maybe a month ago.'

He paused, looking out towards the harbour where machinery and sheds were rapidly disappearing under rampant rainforest regrowth.

'The miners are in the same boat, but they believe they'll eventually be paid. I think their team bosses sent a letter to your dad some weeks ago and they're waiting to hear back, hoping he'll come. They're happy to keep working until they hear because most of them—well, they, we— don't need the money for food or fancy clothes. It just puts the kids through school and university and pays for taking their wives on holidays.'

The words came out fluently enough but Keanu thought he could hear a lingering 'but' behind them.

'But?' Caroline said, and he had to smile that they could still be so much on the same wavelength.

'The miners—they mine. It was the crusher team that did the safety stuff. Your uncle's been putting off staff for months, and he started with the general labourers, saying the bulldozer boys and crusher and extraction operators could do the safety work when the crusher wasn't operating, but now they've gone.'

'Then the miners shouldn't be working,' Keanu said. 'You've got to pull them out of there.'

Reuben shook his head.

'They've got a plan. They're going to stockpile enough rock then come out and work the crusher themselves for a month and that way they can keep the mine going. The miners, they're all from these islands, they know the hospital needs the mine and they need the hospital and the clinics on the islands. Because they're younger, a lot of them have young families—kids. Kids have accidents—need a nurse or a doctor...'

Keanu sighed.

He understood that part of the situation—but nevertheless the mine would have to shut! Safety had to come first and their small hospital just wasn't equipped should a major catastrophe like a mine collapse happen.

Caroline's heart had shuddered at the thought of the miners working in tunnels that might not have been shored up properly, or in water that hadn't been pumped out of the tunnels, but the best way to find out was to talk to them.

'Well, if there are people working here, shouldn't we start the checks?' She turned to Keanu, and read the concern she was feeling mirrored in his eyes. 'How do you usually handle it?'

But it was Reuben who answered her.

'I'll ring through to the team and they send one man out at a time—we do it in alphabetical order so it's easier for you with the files. I'm a bit worried about Kalifa Lui—his cough seems much worse.'

'Should we see him first?' Caroline asked, but Keanu shook his head.

'He'll realise we've picked him out and probably cough

his lungs up on his way out of the mine so his chest's clear when he gets here. Better to keep to the order.'

Reuben had placed a well-labelled accident book in front of Caroline and a box of files on the table where Keanu sat.

Index card files?

Caroline looked around the office—no computer.

Ian's cost-cutting?

She didn't say anything, not wanting to confirm any more Lockhart inadequacies or bring up Ian's name unnecessarily.

Keanu was already flipping through the files, and Reuben was on the phone, organising the check-ups, so Caroline opened the book.

But she was easily distracted.

Looking at Keanu, engrossed in his work, making notes on a piece of paper, leafing back through the files to check on things, she sensed the power of this man—as a man—to attract any woman he wanted. It wasn't simply good looks and a stunning physique, but there was a suggestion of a strong sexuality—maybe more than a suggestion—woven about him like a spider's web.

And she was caught in it.

The memories of their childhood together were strong and bitter-sweet given how it had ended, but this was something different.

'Aaron Anapou, ma'am.'

Jerked out of her thoughts by the deep voice, she looked up to see a dust-smeared giant standing in front of her.

'Ah! Hi! Actually, Keanu's doing the checks. I'm Caroline—I'm the nurse.'

She stood up and held out her hand, which he took gingerly.

'You should have gloves on, ma'am,' he said quietly.

'But then I might miss a little gold dust sticking to my fingers.'

Aware that she'd already held up things for too long, she waved him along the table towards Keanu, who already had the first card in front of him.

Reuben had helpfully laid out the medical implements between the two of them—a stethoscope, ear thermometer and covers, and a lung capacity machine. So what did she do? Act as welcoming committee? Wait for orders?

Behind her desk Reuben had also opened the doors on what looked like a well-stocked medical cabinet.

Maybe she did the dressings.

But, in the meantime, there was the accident book to go through. She looked at the recent pages, then flipped back, interested to see if there were always so few accidents recorded.

It wasn't hard to work out when the crushing and extracting operations had closed down as most of the reported accidents had been caused by some chance contact with some piece of the machinery.

In the background she heard Keanu chiding men for working in flip-flops instead of their steel-capped boots, listened to explanations of water not being pumped out, and her heart ached for the days when the mine had been a well-run and productive place.

'If you're done, you can give me a hand.' Had Keanu guessed she'd been dreaming?

The next miner hadn't tried to hide the fact he'd been working in flip-flops—they were bright green and still on his feet. The skin between his big toe and the second one, where the strap of the sandal rubbed, was raw and inflamed, and a visible cut on his left arm was also infected.

Caroline worked with Keanu now; he cleaned and treated wounds, handing out antibiotics, while she did the lung capacity tests and temperatures.

'I'm surprised there are any antibiotics to give out,' she said when there was a gap between the miners.

'I keep the keys of the chest and no one but me can ever open it,' Reuben said firmly. 'I suppose it was too big for Mr Lockhart to take away and he couldn't break the bolt, although I think he tried.'

Caroline sighed.

Her uncle had left a poisonous legacy behind him on what had once been an island paradise.

And, given her name, she was part of the poison.

'We definitely have to close the mine.' Keanu's voice interrupted her dream of happier times, and she realised the parade of miners—a short parade—from the mine to the table had ceased. 'It would be irresponsible not to do it.'

'And *that* will damage the Lockhart name even more,' Caroline muttered as shame for the trouble her uncle had caused made her cringe.

He touched her quickly on the shoulder. 'We'll talk about it later,' he said, pulling the accident book from in front of her and checking the few notes she'd made.

'Given the state of the mine, there've been remarkably few accidents,' he said. 'Unless, of course…' he looked at Reuben '…you haven't been recording them.'

Reuben's indignant 'Of course I have,' was sincere enough to be believed, especially when he added, 'But remember, not all the men are working. Only this one team at the moment.'

'But even if there haven't been many accidents, that doesn't mean there won't be more in future,' Caroline said, seeing the sense in Keanu's determination that the mine should close.

So what could she do?

Find out whatever she could?

'Reuben, would you mind if I looked at the accounts and wages books?'

He looked taken aback—upset even.

'I'm not checking up on you, but it would help if I could

work out how much the miners are owed. I know Dad would want them all paid. Do you have the wages records on computer?'

'It's all in books, but I keep a copy on my laptop,' Reuben told her, disappearing into the back of the office and returning with the little laptop, handing it over to her with a degree of reluctance.

'We *do* have to close it down,' she admitted to Keanu as they climbed back up the steep steps to the top of the plateau. She was clutching the laptop to her chest.

'You're right,' he said, 'but do you think the men will stop working just because we say so? I'll phone your father—he's the one to do it, and if he can't come over, he can send someone from the Mines Department, someone who might carry some weight with the miners. They could come on Friday's flight.'

Keanu got no answer to his common-sense suggestion. *She's plotting something,* he realised as they climbed back up the steep steps to the top of the plateau.

He knew Caroline in this mood and more often than not whatever she was up to would be either rash or downright dangerous.

But he had worries enough of his own. The elders had placed their faith in him to save the livelihood of the island and the continuation of medical facilities.

'Do we have to go straight back to the hospital or can we sit down with a coffee and work out what to do? I can try to get in touch with Dad,' Caroline said as she led the way towards the house, as if assuming he would agree.

Keanu followed, but hesitated on the bottom step of the big house, his mind arguing with itself.

Of course he could go in—it was just a house, the place where he'd spent so much of his childhood.

Yet his feet were glued to the step.

Caro turned back.

'You're not coming? Do you think we should go back? Bessie would get us some lunch and we could have a talk.'

Then, as if they'd never been apart, she guessed what he was thinking, headed back down to where he stood, took his hand and gently eased him down onto the step, sitting close beside him, her arm around his shoulders.

'Tell me,' she said, and although she spoke softly, it was an order, and suddenly he needed to tell, as if talking about that day would help banish the memories.

He looked out over the island, down towards the sea surrounding it, green-blue and beautiful.

Peaceful...

'I came home on an earlier flight. One kid had measles just before the holidays so they closed a week early. I didn't tell Mum, wanting to surprise her.'

And hadn't he surprised her! The memory of that ugly, desperate scene lived on in his nightmares. He concentrated on the view to block it out of his mind even now...

'I walked up from the plane and into the house. I knew Mum would be in there—dusting or cleaning—she loved the house so much.'

Had Caro heard the break in his voice that her arm tightened around his shoulders?

'They were in the living room, on the floor, on one of your grandma's rugs, like animals.'

He turned to Caroline, needing to see her face, needing to see understanding there.

'I thought he was raping her. I dragged him off, yelling at him, trying to punch him, and...'

'Go on.'

The words were little more than a gentle whisper but now he'd gone this far he knew he had to finish.

'He laughed!' The words exploded out of him, his voice rising at remembered—and still lingering—anger. 'He stood there, pulling up his shorts, buttoning his shirt, and laughed at me. "Do you think she didn't want it?" he said. "Wasn't begging for it? Go on, Helen, tell him how desperate you were to keep what was nothing more than an occasional kindness shag going."'

'Oh, Keanu! I can only imagine how you felt and your poor mother—'

'I lost it, Caro! I went at him, fists flying, while Mum was covering herself and gathering clothes and telling me to stop, not that I did much good. At fifteen I was a fair size, but nothing like Ian's weight. He eventually pushed me to the ground and told me to get out, both of us to get out. He'd ask the plane to wait so we could pack then be out of there.'

'But it was your home, Keanu. It always had been. Grandma had promised that before I was even born!' Caro hauled him to his feet and hugged him properly. 'Anyway, after I arrived Helen was employed by Dad, not Ian.'

Keanu put his hands on her shoulders and eased her far enough apart to look into her face.

'Ian's words destroyed Mum. She refused to talk about it except to say she'd always known she wasn't the only one. I realised then it had been going on for some time. But to humiliate her like that, in front of me—it was more than she could take! When we got back to the house in Cairns she phoned your father to say she wouldn't be there to look after you during the holidays and that she'd retired. No other explanation no matter how often he phoned, even when he visited. With the admiration she had for your father, there was no way she could have told him about it. She just shut herself away from life, then only a few years later she was gone.'

Caro drew him close again, wrapping her arms around him, holding him tightly.

'Oh, Keanu,' she whispered, the words soft and warm

against his neck. 'At least now I understand why you deserted me. How could you have had anything to do with any Lockhart after Ian's behaviour to your mother?'

Was it the release of telling her the story, of her finally knowing why he'd cut her off that made his arms move to enfold her?

He didn't know—he only knew that he held her, clung to her, breathing in the very essence that was Caroline—his Caro. And like a sigh—a breath of wind—something shifted between them…an awareness, tension—

Attraction?

You're married.

Probably.

He didn't actually leap away from her embrace, but the space between them grew.

They were friends, but whatever this new emotion was, it hadn't felt like friendship.

Had Caro felt it?

Were warning bells clanging in her head?

For once he had not the slightest idea of what she was thinking, but deep inside he knew that, whatever lay ahead, he couldn't do anything to hurt her, not again, which meant not getting too involved until he knew he was free.

Something had obviously happened between her and Steve because she was back on the island and he could see she was hurting.

Abandoned again by someone she loved?

Wouldn't he have to do that if his divorce didn't go through?

Get out of here and sort it out!

'You have lunch here,' he said, aiming for sounding calm and composed—sensible—although his whole body churned with emotion. 'I'll go back to the hospital and talk to Sam. He'll know the best way to close down the mine.'

Caroline nodded. 'Yes, good idea.'

Perhaps she hadn't felt what he'd felt when they'd hugged, because she'd never sounded more together—practical, professional—putting the past firmly behind her.

But then, she'd always been a superb actress, having grown adept at hiding her feelings.

Though usually not from him…

CHAPTER SIX

HAD THEY BEEN going to kiss?

Surely not!

But Caroline was very relieved he'd pulled away, and hopefully without seeing her suddenly breathless state.

And if he hadn't?

Would that surge of attraction have led to a kiss—right there on the front steps of the house?

Her heart ached for him after hearing the story of his return from school, his mother's humiliation, and imagining the pain the pair must have suffered, leaving the place that had been their only true home.

Her first reaction had been numbness. After Bessie's chance remark about no woman being safe around Ian, she'd imagined rape, but humiliating Helen as he had done had been emotionally so damaging. How impotent Keanu must have felt in the face of Ian's callousness.

Of course she'd had to hug him!

But hugging Keanu had never felt like that before!

Hugging Keanu had never produced that kind of mayhem in her body. Not even Steve, who'd never failed to boast about what a great lover he was, had ever managed to evoke something like that.

Or was that unfair to Steve?

He hadn't really boasted of his prowess, it was just the

impression she'd got from his confidence, and the fact that other women had envied her the man who had wooed her with flowers, and gifts and promises of undying love.

Actually, now the hurt was gone and she could look back rationally, it had been the undying love thing that had got her in the end; the fact that this person had come into her life, vowing to be there for ever—to never let her down or abandon her. That last had been the clincher.

How stupid had *she* been?

A practised lover, he'd sniffed out the silly issues she had with abandonment—with the loss of so many people in her life and the distraction of others—and had worked on it!

Jilly had been right, she was well out of that relationship, and as the days had turned into months Caroline had realised that as well, glad the man she'd thought she loved had turned out to have not only feet of clay but whole legs of it!

And Keanu?

She closed her eyes and breathed deeply then decided she wouldn't think about that right now. She had more important things to consider, the first being to find some way to pay the miners what they were owed.

She didn't think it would go all the way to restoring the Lockhart name but those people had worked for her family—they deserved to be paid.

And they would be.

She'd phone Dad, talk to him about the mine closure and the problems Ian had left behind him on the island— the damage he had done to the Lockhart name.

Although could she add that much more worry to his already over-burdened shoulders?

An image of her twin rose up in front of her—Christopher's crippled, twisted body, his lovely blue eyes gazing blankly towards her as she talked to him, the pigeon chest battling for every breath...

No, she couldn't pull Dad away from Christopher, especially right now when he had been hospitalised again...

So it was up to her.

Or was she fooling herself?

'Nurse Hettie phoned to say she expected you back at the hospital.' Bessie appeared at the front door. 'I told her you're having a late lunch and will be down soon.'

Bother!

'Thanks, Bessie, I'll go right now.'

'You'll do no such thing. You come into the kitchen and have lunch.'

'But Reuben gave Keanu and I fruit salad and cold juice. I don't need lunch.'

'You do need lunch!'

Realising it was futile to argue, she went into the kitchen to eat the gargantuan sandwich Bessie had prepared for her.

Footsteps on the veranda sent Bessie scurrying from the kitchen, and Caroline carefully wrapped the remainder of the sandwich and popped it into the fridge.

The deep voice she heard was definitely Keanu's.

Her heart made a squiggly feeling in her chest as she hurried to the front veranda.

'There was no need for you to come up, I just had to wash and put on a clean top—it was dusty down there.'

Keanu nodded, just that, a nod, the story he'd shared with her like a glass wall between them.

Or had it been the hug?

Whatever, he'd turned away and started back towards the hospital, pausing only to explain, 'Hettie's done two trips the last two days so she's taking a break, but the patient with the Buruli ulcer needs the skin around it debrided and the wound cleaned, and Anahera has her hands full with the other patients.'

Other patients?

Caroline realised with a start how little she knew about

the hospital and what was going on there. She was a nurse, and the patients should be her first concern, not worrying how to pay the money owed to the miners.

She followed Keanu down the path, ignoring the hitch in her breathing at the breadth of his shoulders and the way his hair curled against the nape of his neck, catching up with him to ask, 'Do we use the treatment room where I first saw him or the operating theatre?

'He doesn't need a full anaesthetic, just locals around the wound, but the theatre is more sterile so we'll do it there.'

Caught up in what lay ahead, Caroline set aside the disturbances Keanu's presence was causing and concentrated on the case.

'Are we using the theatre because the ulcer bacteria are easily transmitted?'

Keanu shook his head.

'We've no idea how it's transmitted, although the World Health Organization has teams of people in various places working on it. Using the theatre is a safeguard, nothing more.'

'And debriding tissue?'

He turned to look at her as they reached the hospital.

'Are you asking questions to prove your worth as a nurse or because you're genuinely interested?'

The deliberate dig took her breath away but before she could get into a fierce, and probably very loud, argument with him, he added, 'I'm sorry, that was unfair. I'm so damned mixed up right now.'

He sighed, dark eyes troubled, then touched her lightly on the shoulder.

'The thing about Buruli is that it produces a toxin called mycolactone that destroys tissue. We have the patient on antibiotics but they are taking time to work, so we're going to clean it up in the hope that we'll kill off any myolactone spores.'

Caroline's mind switched immediately to nurse mode. They'd need local anaesthesia, scalpels, dressings, dishes to take the affected skin to be disposed of in the incinerator.

And she had no idea where that was or, in fact, where any of the other things were kept. Instead of prowling around in the dark with Keanu last night, she should have been checking out the hospital.

She must have sighed, for Keanu said, 'It's okay, Mina will have everything set out for us.'

He *was* still reading her mind!

And, given some of the thoughts flashing through it, that could prove very dangerous—*and* downright embarrassing.

The ulcer was inflamed and looked incredibly painful, but the young man was stoic about it.

Keanu injected local anaesthetic into the tissue around the wound, then checked the equipment while he waited for it to take effect.

'I want to keep as much of the skin intact as I can,' Keanu said, speaking directly to her for the first time. 'I'll trim the edges and try to clean beneath it. I'll need you to swab and use tweezers to clear the damaged bits as I cut.'

Caroline picked up a pair of forceps. The wound was long but reasonably narrow, and she could see what Keanu hoped to do. If he could clean out the wound he might be able to stretch the healthy skin enough to stitch it together.

'If you stitch it up, would you leave a small drain in place?'

He glanced up from his delicate task of scraping and cutting and nodded. Seeing his eyes above the mask he was wearing made her heart jittery again.

This was ridiculous. She was a professional and any interaction between them, at least at the hospital, had to be just that—professional!

She selected another pair of forceps and lifted the skin towards which he was working.

He continued to cut, dropping some bits in one dish and some in a separate one.

Intrigued, she had to ask.

'Why the two dishes?'

He glanced up at her with smiling eyes and any last remnants of hope about professionalism flew out the window—well, there was no window, but they disappeared. That smile re-awoke all the manifestations of attraction that she'd felt earlier, teasing along her nerves and activating all her senses.

'I think I mentioned Sam's a keen bacteriologist,' Keanu was explaining while she told herself she was being ridiculous. 'He's never made Buruli a particular study but he'll be interested to look at it under a microscope. The more people around the world peering at it the better chance we have of developing a defence against it. It's not so bad here in the West Pacific but in some African and Asian nations when it's not treated early it attacks the bone and causes deformities or even loss of limbs.'

'I don't want to lose my leg,' their patient said firmly, and Keanu assured him that no such thing would happen.

'We've got you onto the drugs early enough and once we clean it up you should be fine.'

Keanu was being professional—purely professional.

Until he looked up, caught her eye, and winked.

'I think that's it,' he said, much to her relief. It had been an 'I'm finished' wink, nothing more.

Yet her reaction suggested that keeping things purely professional between herself and Keanu would prove impossible—from her side at least.

No way! She was stronger than that. And she had plenty to occupy her mind. The sooner she could get the back payments for the miners sorted out, and get the mine closed until it could be made safe, the better it would be for the hospital, and if she concentrated on that—

'Okay, I'll get Mina to do the dressing. I think we deserve a coffee.'

She glanced at the clock—they'd been standing over their patient for more than two hours and probably did deserve a coffee.

Well, she could do coffee…

Except he was smiling.

Possibly not.

'What I need more than coffee is a tour of the hospital so I know where everything is and what patient is where. I'll do the dressing then maybe Mina can show me around.'

Keanu could hardly argue, although he could alter the plan slightly.

'Let's stick with Mina doing the dressing and I'll show you around instead.'

Caroline's reaction wasn't what you'd call ecstatic.

More resigned, if anything, but after being distracted by the telling of his mother's distress and their departure from the island earlier, he was hoping to have a chat about the situation at the mine—to find out what she was thinking.

Because she *was* thinking of something she could do to help matters. He'd known her too long and too well not to have picked that up.

But he could hardly ask about it while touring the little hospital and introducing patients, so he'd have to find another time.

'There are four wards, if you can call small two-bed spaces *wards*. Three on this side, with sliding doors that can close each of them off, although most of the time we leave it open for the breezes.'

He led her into the first of these, which, at the moment, had two patients, young men from another island who had taken the tide too lightly and had been injured when the boat they'd been in had overturned on the reef. 'As you can see,' Keanu pointed out, 'one has a broken arm, the other an injured ankle, and both have quite bad coral grazes—'

'Which can easily become infected if not treated promptly and continually.'

Keanu nodded. Anyone who grew up in the islands knew about infections from coral so he wasn't going to give her any brownie points for that. But walking with her, talking with her—even professionally—was so distracting to his body he couldn't help but resent her presence.

If she wasn't here—

No, he was glad she was here.

She belonged here, just as he did. He just had to get over this physical attraction thing.

Be professional.

'The patient in the third bed, in what's technically another ward, you might recognise—Brenko, Bessie and Harold's grandson. The flying surgeon took out his spleen last week after he'd had an accident on his quad bike. More muscle than sense, haven't you?'

The young man grinned, and the patients, who had been quiet as Keanu had brought the stranger into the room, all began to talk at once.

Was she really Caroline Lockhart? How could any Lockhart show her face here? What was going to happen with the mine?

The questions, and the animosity behind some of them, must have hurt Caroline deeply because he heard her sigh with relief when he stopped the talk.

'Caroline is here as a nurse, so if you don't want her jabbing you with unnecessary needles, you'd better start treating her with respect. She's spent more time in these islands than some of you have been alive and is not to blame for anything her uncle did.'

The anger that underlined Keanu's words quietened the

young men, then Brenko said, 'I'm glad you're back, Caroline. I still have the ukulele you gave me when I was little.'

Caroline smiled at the memory, but Keanu guessed that one happy memory wouldn't make up for the animosity that had been thick in the air around her.

He led her through the next small room, this one closed off with the shutters. An elderly woman patient was sleeping soundly, although the young men's voices could be heard quite clearly.

'Unstable diabetic,' Keanu murmured.

'It's the curse of all the Pacific islands,' Caroline replied quietly, and he nodded, then, feeling the hurt he knew she would be nursing, he put his arm around her shoulders and gave her a quick squeeze.

She shot away as if he'd burned her, then must have realised her reaction had been a little extreme and moved close again.

But not close enough for hugs or squeezes, however sympathetic.

In the fourth room, a young woman was sitting up in bed, nursing her baby, Anahera standing by in case either of them needed a bit of help.

'We don't have a maternity ward because we transfer all pregnant women to the mainland at thirty-four to thirty-six weeks, depending on the advice of our flying obstetrician, but this little fellow arrived early,' Keanu explained, smiling at the sight of the mother and child.

'By rights he shouldn't be here. His mum was to be going out on today's flight,' he continued. 'But Hettie and the local midwife who delivered him suspect his dates were wrong. As you can see, he's a good size and he's feeding lustily.'

He turned to smile at Caroline.

'In all truth, we love having him here—we've all gone a bit soft. Because the women and their babies usually fly in and go straight to their homes, we don't get to see the babies except on clinic runs. Consequently, we're happy to keep these two here just in case anything goes wrong. We've got them isolated in this room to keep them clear of any infection.'

'Because you don't know how Buruli ulcers are transmitted?'

'Exactly.'

'The lad with the ulcer will be transferred to the ICU across the passage, beyond the theatre, once Mina has finished dressing the wound. It's next to the recovery room and ICU is probably a grand name for it but it's got a ventilator and monitoring equipment in it. The lad doesn't need it but it does keep him isolated.'

Caroline nodded her understanding.

'We're not finished, are we?' she asked. 'Don't you have linen cupboards and drug cabinets and instruments and sterilisers and a million other things that a hospital, even a small one, needs? Where's your radiography department, for a start?'

'Through here,' he said, moving into a separate wing. 'The theatre you've already seen and all the sterilising stuff is in an annexe off that. Cupboards for sterile clothing, etcetera are also in the annexe, and there's a shower and locker room next to that and beyond the theatre is Radiography.'

'It's well planned,' Caro commented.

'We've your father to thank for that,' he said. 'And him to thank for us having the best and latest in radiography machines. Money from the mine put in the basics—X-ray and ultrasound—and the Australian government donated a mammography machine, but he won a grant from one of the big casinos to put in a CT machine. He really does everything he can for the island and the hospital.'

'The hospital and Christopher,' Caro pointed out, and

Keanu heard the catch in her voice. Did she think her father cared more for the hospital and his son than he did for his daughter?

Keanu remembered that as a child Caro had felt guilty about her mother's death, and Christopher's cerebral palsy, blaming herself for both problems, but there was no way Max would feel that.

'That was bitchy!' she said suddenly. 'Both the hospital and Christopher need him far more than I do. And Dad has so much on his shoulders, the least I can do is understand that and do whatever I might be able to do to lift some of the burden.'

Keanu wanted to argue that she had every right to feel left out, but he wondered if Max's avoidance of the island whenever possible was entirely to do with work and his disabled son, or was it that he was still haunted by his young wife's death?

Would too many heartbreaking memories lay siege to him whenever he was here?

Caro was wandering around the equipment, checking it all.

'So, what do you think?' he asked, dragging his mind from the Lockhart family tragedies to the present.

'It's great equipment for a small hospital but, given the isolation, I'd say it's all necessary. And I can see why Dad's been working his butt off, not only for money to keep the place afloat but doing all the lobbying with business and government.'

The way she spoke told Keanu she saw little of her adored father, but as he watched she shrugged off whatever she was thinking and tugged at one of the curtains that screened off various sections of the room.

She poked her head out from behind the curtain and grinned cheekily, doing terrible things to Keanu's heart, lungs, not to mention his determination to keep things professional between them.

'We didn't think of all of this when we decided to become the doctor and the nurse on Wildfire, did we?'

'Didn't know "all this" existed,' Keanu reminded her, hoping he sounded more in control than he felt.

Trying to get her and the past out of his mind, he remembered the look on her face as they'd come back from the mine and his wanting to find out what she was up to.

'The laundry cupboards and other stuff are closer to the kitchen and even if you don't want a coffee, I do.'

She followed him obediently, said hello to the cook when he introduced them, then politely but adamantly refused to answer any questions.

'To tell you the truth, Keanu, I have no idea what I can do to sort out all that's happened at the mine, but I know I have to do something. The hospital needs a functioning mine, and the islands need the hospital, so we can't just let it all fizzle out. Besides, it was a Lockhart who caused all the problems, so it's up to me to at least try to do something to sort it out.'

But what?

The question bugged him, to the extent that he found himself, much later, when all was well in the hospital and Sam and Hettie both on call, walking up the hill, skirting the lagoon, to the house where he'd grown up.

They'd grown up.

He climbed the steps but once again hesitated on the veranda, reluctant to go in.

'Caro?'

His call was tentative—pathetic, really.

'If you want to see me you'll have to come in,' she yelled from somewhere inside, and he guessed from the direction of her voice that she'd be sitting at the big table in the dining room, pen and paper at hand, trawling through the information on the laptop.

Of course he could go in. It had been his home as much as hers, and although as a Lockhart she probably had more rights, his mother had run the place for years.

Until...

Then Caro was there, so much sympathy in her eyes he thought his heart might crack.

She put both arms around him and drew him close.

'I know it must be dreadful, having to walk through here again, but I'm in the dining room, and you have to do it some time. Standing out here isn't going to banish the memory, now, is it?'

Her hair touched his shoulder, soft as silk, and the woman smell of her filled his head with fantasy.

So much so, his arms returned her hug until it became more than a hug and they were kissing—gentle, exploratory kisses that nonetheless sent fire throughout his body and a throbbing need deep inside it.

Eventually—fortunately—she eased away.

'Well, that was weird,' she said lightly, before leading him firmly into the house.

But it was more than weird, it was dangerous. The attraction he was feeling was obviously mutual, but there were so many ifs and buts about it...

She'd led him into the dining room, and Keanu looked at the bits of paper scattered across the shining surface.

'What on earth are you doing?' he demanded.

'I'm trying to work out exactly how much the workers are owed, and once I know that I'd like to know how much it costs to run the mine on a weekly or monthly basis.'

'And then you'll know how much you need to win on Lotto to fix everything up,' Keanu finished for her.

She glared at him.

'You may mock, but while it might be hard to find

money for projects like this, it would be impossible if we don't know what we need. If I can work out a kind of ball-park figure, we can take it from there—get some investors, speak to banks, big businesses, whatever. It might be beyond us whatever we do, but at least we'd know we tried.'

Keanu understood what she was saying and a tiny spark of light flickered in his brain. The seed of an idea he couldn't yet grasp.

Kind of hard to grasp at glimmers of ideas in his head when most of it was occupied with telling his body that a sympathy kiss from Caroline meant nothing, and the fact that his body was attracted to hers was probably nothing more than their closeness in their childhood, and he was still married...

Probably.

Was she feeling the awkwardness too, that she suddenly bundled up all her bits of paper into a very rough pile and said, 'The moon's up, let's go for a walk. I haven't been down to the lagoon since I got back—there always seems to be something else to do.'

She made it sound like a peaceful stroll down to one of their favourite childhood places, but his body screamed at him to resist at all costs. The moon was not just up, it was full. The lagoon would be bathed in its soft glow, as would the woman with whom he was strolling.

But when had he ever been able to say no to Caro?

Once outside, in the light of the said moon, Caroline realised what a stupid idea it had been. Bad enough that she'd already been kissing Keanu, kissing him and wanting to keep kissing him. It was more than weird, it was scary.

But wonderful.

That thought filled her with a kind of awe...

And how was she going to cope with Keanu *and* moonlight, twin attractions, twin magic?

But she could hardly back off now, so she strode down the slightly overgrown path they'd used as children towards the end of the lagoon just above the small waterfall, where a large, flat rock only inches above the level of the water gave a wonderful view, not only of the entire lake but of the village beneath the plateau.

Keanu caught up with her as she reached the thicker rainforest that protected the waterhole, reaching out a hand to steady her as the track was rough. Roots and vines conspired to catch at their feet and they brushed against each other often.

Definitely not one of her better ideas.

The touch of his hand had been enough, but skin on skin contact, no matter how accidental, had made goose-bumps rise on her arms and neck as her nerve endings battled with the notion that this was Keanu—just a friend!

They reached the lagoon, and trod carefully around its rocky edge towards the small opening through which the water tumbled its way down a rocky path to the flat land below.

And there was their rock. Caroline hurried on, anxious to be there as if sitting in such a familiar place would protect her from all the unfamiliar reactions she was getting from being around her old friend.

But once he'd joined her she realised the rock had shrunk.

Ridiculous, they had grown, so now they sat, close together, feet flat, knees raised, hands looped around their legs.

Very close together!

And in spite of the moonlight, the lagoon looked dark and mysterious, the surface silvered, but with a sense of hidden depths lurking beneath that shining skin.

Hidden depths...

The man beside her would have those too, not deliberately hidden but ideas, emotions, even ethics and beliefs that developed with maturity so for all she thought she knew him, she really didn't.

'I have got one idea to get the money,' she said tentatively, as the side of her body closest to Keanu heated towards fever level. 'Do you remember Dad explaining to us—well, to me, I suppose, but I'm sure you were there—that my mother's parents had left their house in Sydney jointly to Christopher and me? They'd also left most of their money, which was apparently considerable, in trust for Christopher and the interest on that pays for his full-time carers and the housekeeper and upkeep on the house.'

She leant forward so a curtain of hair saved her from looking at Keanu's face. Studying it in the moonlight that picked out the strong bones of his cheeks and jaw, the straight line of his nose was just too distracting.

'I vaguely remember, but is this story going somewhere?' Keanu replied, moving slightly and tucking her protective curtain back behind her ears, presumably so he could see her face, for he'd turned to study her at the same time.

She felt the brush of his fingers as he moved her hair, could feel his eyes on her skin—soft eyes, gentle, understanding, like a caress…

'Well, it might be—it *could* be a solution,' she said, her voice wavering as her body reacted to his gaze, *and* realised just how stupid this was all going to sound. 'I thought if I could borrow enough money by mortgaging my half of the house, we might just be able to get the mine working again and eventually there'd be money over and above what it pays to the hospital for me to repay the loan.'

He hesitated for a moment, then slipped his arm around her shoulders, as if preparing her for a hug when he disappointed her with his reply.

'Caro…' His voice was deep and husky and his arm

tightened around her shoulders. 'I know you said it was your first idea, but if you don't mind my saying so, it isn't the best idea you've ever had. What if we can't get the mine going again, and the bank forecloses and Christopher loses his home?'

'But surely they'd...' Caroline protested, so flustered by Keanu's touch she'd forgotten what she'd meant to say.

'Only take half a house?' Keanu finished for her, showing just how ridiculous the idea had been.

Had she looked so disappointed that Keanu used the arm around her shoulders to pull her closer? A comforting hug, nothing more, but given where her comforting hug to him had led earlier, she really should pull away.

Except it *was* comforting.

Too comforting...

For Keanu too, as he suddenly let his arm slip and got back to practicalities?

'Now, as you were right about knowing a ballpark figure for the amount of money we need,' he said, 'let's go back to your notes and see what we can come up with.'

He stood up, reaching down to help her to her feet, then keeping her hand in his, not exactly imprisoned because she knew she could pull hers out but firmly, as if he wanted it there.

Here she went again, feeling things between her and Keanu when in reality it was nothing more than their old friendship.

Back in the house, she made tea, and put out biscuits Bessie had cooked that day, carrying them through to the dining room where Keanu was already going through her figures.

Or would have been if he hadn't been holding the old notebook she'd pulled out of her room to use the blank pages in it, running his fingers over the hearts and flowers she'd drawn on the cover—the hearts with the arrow running through them, linking her initials to his.

She snatched it out of his fingers.

'It's the first thing I could find to write on,' she muttered. 'But to get back to the mine, the closest I've got to a total is the wages owed and the full wages for running the mine—from figures back when Peter was here. I just need weekly or monthly running costs from Reuben and we'll have some idea of what's needed.

'We can get them later,' Keanu assured her, taking the book from her but flipping back to the cover of the book and smiling at her. The teasing warmth of that smile sent ripples of what felt very like desire downwards through her body.

'I was ten, just look at the figures!' she snapped, but he kept smiling.

Damn the man. It was just so much easier being near him when he wasn't smiling.

But they stood up together, the air between them dense with tension.

In the end it was he who broke the spell, stepping back, so they stood, a foot apart, still looking into each other's eyes.

Then Keanu smiled, and she regretted the foot of space between them, because right then there'd be nothing she'd have liked more than to be locked in his arms.

Locked in his arms?

As in romance?

'You loved me when you were ten,' he reminded her, before turning and walking quietly out of the room, down the hall, across the veranda and down the steps.

Gone...

CHAPTER SEVEN

AS HE'D MENTIONED, Keanu was off duty, and Anahera and an aide Caroline didn't know were working in the hospital when Caroline arrived the next morning.

'Sam's in his office,' Anahera told her. 'And Hettie says she's taking a day off, which she should, but I bet she's doing paperwork in her little villa—she finds it hard to stop, although she does love exploring the island, swimming in the lagoon and climbing around the waterfall. She has a true passion for this place.'

'And you?' Caroline asked, glad to have an opportunity to chat with Anahera even if they were only counting drugs in the dangerous drugs cabinet.

Anahera didn't answer for a moment, then, to Caroline's surprise, she said, 'Well, me, I'm just glad you've turned up. The island is my home and I'm happy here with Hana, but since Keanu's arrival, Mum's been trying to push us both together.'

'Not interested?' Caroline said as casually as she could.

'Once bitten, twice shy,' Anahera answered obliquely. 'Not that being interested in Keanu would do me any good. Even Mum's realised how he is around you.'

Caroline felt heat in her cheeks.

'It's just because we've always known each other,' she said, then realised how lame she'd sounded.

The drugs all counted and checked off on the list taped on the cabinet door, the pair of them walked through the hospital.

'Do you want to change the dressings on the coral cuts while I do some bloods?'

It was good to be doing routine nursing work and now they'd accepted her, the lads with the coral cuts were fun. She took off the old dressings, cleaned the wounds, which were looking good, applied antibiotic ointment and covered them again.

By the next day, she guessed, they'd be able to go home.

She and Anahera had a coffee in the kitchen with a slice of extremely good hummingbird cake, and were just finishing it when Keanu appeared.

'Can you come down to the airstrip?' he asked, bypassing any politeness. 'There's an emergency call-out to Atangi. Hettie's done two flights the last two days so Sam suggested you come along to see what we do.'

You'll be okay, just don't touch him more than necessary, the sane voice in her head said firmly, but the professional part of her mind was focussed firmly on what lay ahead.

'What kind of an emergency?' she asked.

Keanu was hurrying beside her now, long strides eating up the ground.

'Pregnant woman, thirty weeks, having severe cramps.'

He paused—both feet and words—and turned to look at Caroline.

'We'll see how she is when we get there, maybe just bring her back here. Atangi's a good clinic for you to see first, as it has a fairly well-equipped and stocked operating theatre. Before the hospital was built, the flying doctors used it for their emergency visits.'

'Thirty weeks, so we'll take a humidicrib and resus gear?'

'Already in the chopper.'

They'd reached the airstrip, where Sam was talking to Jack.

'You're okay to do this?' Sam asked, looking at Caroline.

'Very okay,' Caroline assured him, not adding that she was actually excited at the thought of going to Atangi after so long a time. You could hardly tell your boss you were excited that someone was ill.

The flight was short, but so beautiful it brought tears to Caroline's eyes. The translucent green water over the reefs, the deeper blue of the sea between the islands, then there was the harbour at Atangi.

'Did you remember Alkiri telling us about the harbour being blasted through the coral by the Americans during the Second World War?' Keanu asked as they dropped down to land on a marked circle next to a building Caroline recognised as the clinic.

As children, she and Keanu had been brought here for their immunisations, and occasionally treated by the resident nurse for minor injuries.

'It seems funny, being back,' she said as she followed Keanu out of the helicopter, feeling a now-familiar tension as his hand held her arm to steady her.

Keanu leaned back in to pull out a backpack, and Caroline knew it would contain all the emergency equipment they might need.

'The clinic is actually well stocked and we probably won't need anything apart from the mobile ultrasound unit that's in here, but it's just as easy to take the lot.'

He spoke to Jack, who'd shut down the engine and disembarked, carrying the portable humidicrib and another bag of equipment.

'You'll stand by?'

Jack shifted uneasily from one foot to the other.

'Actually, I'd like to take a look at the engine. It was missing a bit on the way over, which sounds as if a little moisture has got into the Avgas. Last night was cooler than we've had and the supply tank I used to refuel was close to empty so there could have been some condensation in it.'

'Which means?' Caroline asked, pleased she hadn't heard the missing beat of the engine.

'I'll drain the tank—get an empty drum from the store to put it into—and refill the chopper tank here. We keep a small tanker of Avgas here because we often need to re-fuel, and it's useful if we're doing search-and-rescue work, which is co-ordinated from here.'

'How long?' Keanu asked.

'Three hours tops,' Jack replied cheerfully.

Three hours! They wouldn't be rushing the pregnant woman back to Wildfire.

Keanu introduced the local nurse, Nori, the name re-minding Caroline they'd been at school together. They hugged and exchanged greetings, although Keanu broke up the very brief reunion with a reminder that they had a patient.

Their patient was standing in a corner of an examination room, bent over and clinging to the table. A large woman, it was hard to tell she was actually pregnant.

'Baby's coming,' she said as they came in. 'Soon.'

'Are you able to get up on the table so I can examine you?' Keanu asked in his deep, caring voice.

'No way! I'm not getting up there. The baby's com-ing now.'

Nori was plugging in the crib to warm the mattress in it, and fitting an oxygen tube to the inlet, so Caroline grabbed a small stool that seemed to have no apparent purpose and pulled it over so Keanu could squat on it while he felt the woman's stomach for the strength of the contractions.

Nori had laid out clean towels, gloves and various instruments on a trolley beside the table. Caroline put on gloves, took a towel, just in case the baby did come unexpectedly, and checked that suction tubes and scissors were among the instruments.

If the baby popped out limp, they would have to resuscitate it, but at least they had the humidicrib to keep it pink and warm on the way back to Wildfire.

Keanu was talking quietly to the woman in their own language, and Caroline knew enough of it to know it was mainly reassurance, although he slipped in a question from time to time. Apparently this was her sixth child, so she probably knew more about childbirth than either she or Keanu.

She was thinking this when the woman gave a loud cry and squatted lower, Caroline getting her hands down quickly enough as a watery mix of fluid rushed out.

The baby followed, straight into Caroline's waiting hands—sure and steady hands, although inside she was a mix of trepidation and elation.

The little one cried out, protesting her abrupt entry into the world but with her little fat hands clutching the umbilical cord as if she was ready to take on whatever it had to offer her.

Certainly not a thirty-week baby, more like thirty-six, perhaps even full term.

Keanu reached out a hand to help Caroline and her precious bundle up from the floor, then took the child and passed her to her mother.

The look of love and joy on the woman's face as the baby nuzzled at her breast brought tears to Caroline's eyes.

Keanu was clamping the cord, ready to cut it, but the woman took the scissors out of his hand.

'I do this for my babies,' she told him, cutting cleanly between the clamps.

She passed the baby back to Caroline, who put her down

gently on the table on a warm sheet Nori had taken from the crib. Carefully, she wiped the tiny baby clean, suctioned her nostrils and mouth, Keanu taking over for the Apgar score, then Nori produced another warm sheet and Caroline swaddled the little girl, whose rosebud lips were pursing and opening like a goldfish's, instinct telling her she should be attached to her mother's breast.

Yet Caroline's arms felt reluctant as she passed the baby back, which was ridiculous.

As if arms even knew what reluctance was...

Nori led the woman to a comfortable armchair and said she'd take care of things from now.

Caroline made to argue but Keanu shook his head, just slightly, and led her out of the clinic.

'The islanders have their own rituals for disposing of the placenta,' he explained as they stood in the sun, feeling it warm on their skin after the cool of the air-conditioning inside. 'Before the hospital the islanders had their own midwife—sometimes two—who cared for all the pregnant women. When you and Christopher were born, your father called for one of these women but it was beyond her ability to save either Christopher from injury, or your mother. Your father then decided that all women should have their babies on the mainland and when young women went to the mainland for training as nurses, the midwives stopped passing on their skills.'

'But now?' Caroline asked. 'Seems to me someone having their sixth baby wouldn't have got the dates wrong—and then there's the baby who was in hospital when I arrived.'

'Exactly,' Keanu replied with a grin that made her stupid heart race. 'Now they have the hospital and helicopter as back-up, I think they've decided with a little cheating they can have an island birth. In fact, one of the local nurses is over in Sydney, doing some advanced midwifery training.

It might not be traditional midwifery but at least, when she returns, the island women will have the option of staying here.'

'Which is wonderful,' Caroline declared, smiling herself at the remembered feel of the little baby dropping into her hands. 'So now?' she added, feeling that standing in the sun smiling inanely was probably making her look like an idiot. 'Can we go for a walk? It is so long since I was on Atangi, I need to get the feel and smell of the place back into my blood.'

Keanu swallowed a huge sigh.

He could hardly say no. The baby was fine and whatever was going on inside the clinic was islander business—and women's business at that.

The problem was that the look on Caro's face as she'd stared in wonder at the baby she'd caught had stirred all kinds of uncomfortable thoughts in his mind, and unease in his body.

He'd felt tension from Caro's closeness the whole time they had been in the room and although he was professional enough to not let it affect him, now he wasn't fully focussed on something else, the awareness had grown.

It was because of the notebook, and something to do with sitting on the rock and feeling her hurt when he'd pointed out the flaws in her idea—feeling her disappointment, although she was smart enough to know it would never have worked. Up until then, he'd been able to explain away his physical reactions to her by the fact she was an attractive woman—nothing more than normal physical reactions.

But this was Caro…

'I *can* go for a walk by myself,' she said, obviously sensing his hesitation.

Get over it, he told himself.

'No, it'll be an hour before Jack finishes his refuelling,' he said to her. 'Why don't you wander down to the harbour while I go and see a couple of the elders about Alkiri's funeral?'

She hesitated, and he wondered if she was feeling the same awkwardness that was humming through his nerves.

'Come with me or I'll come with you,' she said quietly. 'Let's be friends again.'

He heard the plea in her voice and a faint tremor in the words caused a pain in his chest.

'Can we just be friends?' he asked.

Fire sparked in her eyes.

'Oh, for heaven's sake, Keanu, I don't know that any more than you do. But there's stuff that needs to be done, things we can do to help the situation here, so surely we can get over all that's happened between us in the past and this inconvenient attraction business that's happening now and work together to make things better.'

She paused, then added in a quieter voice, 'Our friendship was special to me and, I think, to you. Maybe the reward for our efforts would be finding that again.'

He put his arm around her shoulders and drew her close although every functioning brain cell was yelling at him to keep his distance.

The lovely eyes he knew so well looked into his—wary and questioning.

'Our friendship was the most important thing in my life, Caro,' he admitted. 'That will never change.'

She half smiled and shifted so her body wasn't touching his—apart from his arm, which still rested on her shoulders.

'Thanks,' she said, and moved away completely, then in a tone that told him any emotional talk between them was done she added, 'Let's go and see the school first.'

But that was a mistake.

The first thing they noticed—everyone noticed—in the schoolyard was the huge old curtain fig tree, so called because air roots grew down from the branches, forming a thick curtain around the trunk.

And behind that curtain, like hundreds of children who'd attended the school over the years, they'd once shared a very chaste kiss. Her grandma had died and Caroline had known they'd both be off to mainland schools the following year, and for some reason—playing hide and seek most probably—they'd both ended up beneath the fig.

Not that an innocent kiss between a ten-year-old girl and a twelve-year-old boy meant much, but the memory sent a tingle up her spine.

'All the kids are in school,' Keanu murmured. 'Should we?'

Of course they shouldn't but she was ducking between the trailing roots right behind him, letting him take her in his arms, turn her towards him, and lift her head to his, to relive that first kiss.

In actual fact, it was nothing like that first kiss, more like a first kiss between two people attracted to each other and early on in the courtship.

Tentative, exploring, tasting and then tempting, Keanu felt heat rise in his body, and strained to keep things—well, not exactly casual, more noncommittal, if such a thing was possible.

When Caro began kissing him back as if her life depended on the joining of their lips, the contact of their tongues...

Or was it he who'd intensified things—he couldn't think straight, could barely think at all, except that there was no way he should be kissing Caro like this when his life was such a mess.

It was a silly, sentimental thing to do, but there was nothing silly or sentimental about the way their lips met, the teasing invasion of Keanu's tongue, her own tangling with it, the heat in his body as her hands pushed up his shirt to touch his skin, no doubt matched by the heat in hers as his hand slid down her neck towards her breast.

A hundred questions jumbled in her head. Was this just attraction? Or perhaps leftover love from their youth? And hadn't attraction led her into trouble with Steve? No, she could answer that one honestly—it had been his attention to her that had made her lose her head with Steve.

But this kiss—this kiss was different. This kiss was amazing—

So why was she so bamboozled?

'Damn it all!'

The explosive words broke the spell.

'I thought we were trying to be friends,' he muttered, taking her hand and almost dragging her out from under the tree. 'Do you realise I could have made love to you right there under the tree with half of Atangi walking by? Why on earth would you kiss me back like that?'

'Oh, so it's all my fault?' Caroline retorted. 'Anyway, we're both adults and if we feel like it, why shouldn't we kiss?'

She could feel the heat in her cheeks, the disappointment and relief battling for supremacy in her body.

Not that he'd know it because she was stalking away from him, throwing back over her shoulder, 'Anyway, it was your fault—you started it!'

But hearing the words they'd flung at each other so often in childhood fights, she felt a deep sorrow for all they'd lost...

Or had they?

What about the friendship they'd decided to rediscover?

'Nice walk?' Nori asked brightly when they returned to the clinic, any further exploration totally forgotten.

'It had its moments,' Caroline replied, then proceeded

to ask Nori about her family, marital status and children, a conversation that lasted until Jack returned to tell them they could head back to Wildfire.

Not interested in the brilliance Nori's three-year-olds were already showing, Keanu had moved into the theatre to check their patient. She was dozing in the big chair, the baby sleeping against her breast.

The sight brought unexpected emotion welling up inside him, bringing a thickness to his throat.

Time he was out of there...

'Coming back with us?' Keanu said to Caro, who was still deep in a conversation about Nori's children.

Which made him wonder as she said, 'Yes, sir!' and followed him out of the clinic, why she'd never married the Steve guy and had children of her own.

Apart from their medical ambitions, if he remembered rightly they had been going to get married and have ten children.

Ten?

'Did you know Nori has six children—three sets of twins?'

Keanu shook his head. She'd been talking to Nori—talking about children—so it was a fairly innocuous thing for Caro to have said. But coming right on top of the thick throat and his memory of the past, it shook him. There were far too many things going on his head that he didn't want her picking up on, although he wouldn't have minded having a few clues about her thoughts.

Fortunately, by the time they arrived back on Wildfire he had an excuse to escape. He had to concentrate on the arrangements for Alkiri's funeral and the first thing on the list was to try entry to the research station via the gate, and get permission from whoever was in charge.

Should he ask Caroline to accompany him?

She'd been anxious to know what was happening at the station but walking with her through the scented tropical dusk with her was too much to contemplate.

He went in to see Sam, inevitably battling paperwork in his office, to check he wasn't needed at the hospital.

'You're free to go, mate,' Sam told him, 'and I've already got their okay. In fact, the bloke who's the foreman down there actually contacted me to see if I'd like to come down and see the laboratories, and I asked him about the longhouse. But if you want to check it out, just explain who you are to the gate people. Sounded to me that, now they've finished, they're happy to have people see what they've achieved.'

Sam's eyes slid away from his, and Keanu turned to see Caroline standing there.

'You want to go with Keanu and see the renovations down the road?'

'We're allowed in?' She sounded so delighted Keanu could hardly say he didn't want her with him.

'As of today,' Sam was assuring her.

At least she wouldn't be wearing a wet shift, Keanu told himself, but somehow that wasn't comforting at all. She'd been in the same mid-calf pants and uniform shirt when they'd kissed under the tree...

The foreman's name was Bill and he was at the gate talking to the guard there when Keanu and Caroline arrived.

'Sorry about the fence, but the boss wanted the place secure—or as secure as anything can be with so much beach frontage. It was mainly to keep out adventurous kids during the building process, and the fences and guard will remain because the laboratories will have some evil chemicals in them. Not that they won't be locked as well, and I imagine there'd be more kids coming by boat than down from the hospital, but what he says goes.'

'Who is he?' Caroline asked, so excited to be 'invited' to the station that she was barely registering Keanu by her side.

Well, almost barely.

'Some fellow from the Middle East apparently. I get my orders from his—what do they call him?—Australasian manager. He's from the Middle East as well, but speaks English the same way the Queen does.'

Caroline smiled. Children from all over the world were educated in top English public schools so undoubtedly all of them spoke 'like the Queen does'.

Keanu was talking to Bill, so Caroline dawdled behind them, trying to identify all the different scents. She saw the jasmine creeping up the fence—soon it would be smothered—and the broad leaves of the ginger plant, their drooping white bulb-like flowers giving out what was probably her favourite perfume. Or did she prefer the frangipani that was dominant now—?

'You with us?' Keanu asked, and she realised how far she'd fallen back. He and Bill were at the door of the newly renovated and freshly painted laboratory block.

She caught up as Bill unlocked the door, and she gasped at the difference. Admittedly, it had been thirteen years since she'd been in the lab—back when she'd had her last holiday here with Keanu and Helen.

After they left it had never been the same and she'd used the excuse of spending more time with Christopher to avoid island holidays.

'It's been completely redone,' Keanu was saying. 'No wonder Sam's so excited about it. But do you know if there are people booking to come here to use it?'

Bill shook his head.

'Not my department, but we have been hurrying to finish everything and be out of the way because the boss—the big boss—is planning some kind of exclusive, very clever scientists' get-together some time soon.'

They went to check the longhouse next, and once again Caroline could only gape in amazement. Rebuilt in the style of the island meeting places, thatched roof—probably with something underneath the palm thatching to stop it leaking—and open on all sides, it was finished with the best of materials, with cedar benches polished to a glowing shine, weavings hanging from the rafters, mats and cushions strewn around the floor. It was an island longhouse for today and for the future.

'It's totally awesome,' she said, shaking her head because it was hard to take it all in.

'And we can use it for Alkiri's funeral feast?' Keanu asked, as if he already knew this had been agreed.

'Sure thing,' Bill said. 'It will be a good test of the fire pits.'

'It's even got fire pits?'

She sounded so incredulous both men smiled, but she followed them beyond the building where, sure enough, a deep pit had been dug with a more shallow one beside it, big stones, firewood and white sand stored neatly in the bottom of open wooden cupboard-like structures beside it.

'We've had some of the local community here, doing the mats and cushions, and they told us about the fire pits. A big one for the fire that heats the stones, then a shallower one for the stones to go into when they're hot, baskets for the food and bags and sand to cover it all up. Have we got it right?'

He was obviously anxious, but Keanu clapped him on the back and said, 'Fantastic, mate, it's just fantastic.'

Caroline had opened one of the top cupboards and found the baskets for the food stacked inside it. The next one held the sacks that would be wet and placed across the food before the lot was covered with sand to keep the heat in and help the meal steam-cook.

The thought that she'd actually be here and celebrating with a *hangi* made her turn to Keanu in delight.

'Won't it be great? It's so long since we've been to a *hangi*!'

'Great if we don't have to cook it,' Keanu reminded her, but Bill assured them both that local staff had already been employed for the station and they were bringing in more people for the celebration of Alkiri's life the following day.

'Apparently people will come from all the islands, and as we're leaving soon, it will be kind of a reward for our workers to be here for the party.'

Bill hesitated then added, 'Although that sounds a bit rough, partying when someone's dead.'

'Not here,' Keanu assured him. 'Here we celebrate a life that enriched all who knew him—or her if it's a woman's funeral.'

Bill seemed content, but Caroline considered what he'd said.

Had *she* enriched anyone's life?

She rather doubted it.

Christopher's maybe.

He'd certainly enriched hers, getting through each day of pain and illness with a smile always ready on his face for her or their father. During the 'Steve years' as she was starting to think of them, she'd seen less of her brother and really regretted it. Love, or what she'd thought was love, had made her selfish.

They were walking back up to the hospital while these thoughts coursed through her head.

'You okay?' Keanu asked, and she realised she'd dropped behind again, drifting through the past.

Which, considering the confusion she was feeling in *his* presence, might have been a safer place.

'Fine,' she lied, and hurried to catch up with him.

CHAPTER EIGHT

IT WAS A day without end, or so it seemed to Caroline when they returned to the hospital.

'Would you mind keeping an eye on things while Keanu, Hettie and I have some dinner?' Sam greeted her. 'Hettie's cooking because Vailea's already preparing for the funeral feast and there's stuff the three of us have to go over, including juggling the roster for the funeral tomorrow.'

'No worries,' Caroline assured him, 'though you'd better tell me what to do in an emergency. Do I go to the back door and yell?'

'Oh, you don't know the system? Of course not, you've barely arrived and we haven't stopped working you. See the panel by the door? It was an ingenious idea worked out by your father. You hit the blue button for me—it rings in my room—the green for Hettie—and the red that will clang all through the villas for all hands on deck.'

'No fire alarm?' Caroline teased, and Sam pointed to the regulation fire alarm box set beside the panel.

'Open that one and press the button and they'll hear you over on Atangi! And the village will have men here almost as fast as the staff can get here. The hospital's very important to all the islanders—and they've your father to thank for that.'

Caroline thought the conversation was over, until Sam

added, almost under his breath, 'Although we'd prefer to be thanking him in person.'

'My father loves the island. All M'Langi. I can hear it in his voice when he talks about it, asks questions. But my mother's death, and Christopher… It seems he blamed himself, and now he says both the hospital and Christopher need him more on the mainland. Over there he can keep a watch on Christopher's care and also make money and lobby for money to keep this place going.'

Sam sighed and departed, but the conversation had brought Caroline's mind back to the problems at the mine. Of course mortgaging half a house had been a stupid idea, but Keanu hadn't come up with anything better.

Keanu…

The kiss…

Setting the past and the future firmly out of her mind, she went into the big ward, where she discovered that the boys with the coral cuts had been released. The woman with unstable diabetes was sleeping once again, as was their patient with the Biruli ulcer. The woman with the baby had also gone, so all she had to do was hang around in case she was needed.

And use the time to try to sort out the mess inside her head.

Start with the mine—there had to be *some* way…

But how could she think when she was hungry? She headed for the kitchen, where she found several salads made up in the main refrigerator.

'Staff salads,' the note attached to the shelf said, so she took one, went back into the desk in the ward to keep an eye on her patients and ate it there.

Thinking, almost subconsciously, of the grandparents she'd barely known.

How terrible for them to have lost their daughter—their only child—so far away from home. Max had flown his wife's body back to Sydney to be buried there, and had taken first his babies, and later his toddlers—well, Christopher had never actually toddled—to visit their grandparents.

But both of them had been dead before Caroline was six so it was difficult for her to summon up more than an image of a defeated-looking old man and woman.

Defeated by grief, she'd realised, much later.

'Are you okay? You must be tired. I can take over here if you like.'

Keanu's arrival interrupted her unhappy thoughts.

'No way. I have a feeling if I handed over, or even had you standing by, it would reinforce everyone's opinion of the worthlessness of all Lockharts.'

Keanu smiled, something she wished he wouldn't do, at least when she was around.

'Hettie will be over soon and she'll stay until Mina comes on, but I can at least hang around and keep you company. I'm being Maddie this week and she was on call so I might as well be here.'

He pulled a chair over from beside the wall and sat beside her at the small desk, far too close.

Caroline managed to manoeuvre her chair a little farther away from him but he was still too close. She could feel the force-field of him, as if the very air around him had taken on his essence. It was because of the kiss—she knew that. It had done something to her nerves and spun threads of confusion through her head.

'I talked to your father,' he said, startling her out of thoughts of kisses and physical closeness. 'He can't get over at the moment but has asked me to make sure the mine is closed, at least temporarily until he gets a chance to look at things and maybe get it going again.'

'*You* talked to Dad?'

'I thought it might be easier, the mine closure, coming from me and not a Lockhart. I know how distressed you are about the damage Ian's done to the family name.'

Caroline turned so she could study him.

'And you think you telling them will make a difference? It's still the Lockhart mine, and with everyone connected to it now losing their incomes, of course the blame will come back on the Lockharts.'

She was so upset she had to stand up—to move—pacing up and down the silent ward while her mind churned.

It was the right thing to do—she knew that. It was far too dangerous for the miners to keep working without the tunnel being shored up.

'I'll do it,' she said, suddenly weary of the whole mess, and when Keanu started to argue she even found a tired smile.

'Best all the blame lands on us,' she told him. 'We don't want everyone hating you as well.'

Keanu shot up from his chair and took her hands.

'No one will ever blame you, Caroline,' he said, and the feel of her hands in his—the security of her slim fingers being held by his strong ones—fired all her senses once again.

She eased away from him.

'I have patients to check, and it's probably best if you go, because it's too easy to be distracted when you're around.'

'Really?'

He smiled as if she'd given him a very special gift, then leaned forward to peck her cheek before leaving the room.

Keanu went back to his quarters but was too restless to settle down. His phone call to Max, the closing of the mine and his still-vague idea of how to save it, his increasing attraction to Caroline—all were drawing him further and further into the web that was the Lockharts.

He couldn't help but think of his mother, so humiliated by Ian.

Probably already ill, she'd never really overcome their banishment from the island. It was as if Ian's words had left an enduring scar in her mind, and poison in her body. In his mother's mind, the happy Lockhart days had gone, and the stories of the Lockharts taking her in after her own family had disowned her and her husband had died had been long forgotten.

Almost without orders from his brain, his feet took him back out of the villa that was currently his home and up the hill to the grassy slope behind the big house to where his father was buried among dead Lockharts and other islanders who'd lived and worked on Wildfire.

To the grassy slope where Alkiri would be laid to rest tomorrow…

Keanu sat down by his father's grave, idly pulling a few weeds that had recently appeared, trying desperately, as he often did, to remember his father.

But memories of a two-year-old were dim and not particularly reliable so all he had were the stories his mother had told over the years.

His father, bright star of the school on Atangi, had been sent to the mainland for his high-school education, all the costs met by the Lockhart family. From boarding school he'd gone on to university, studying science, and returning, with the woman he'd met and fallen in love with, to Wildfire to work at the research station and begin the first investigation into the properties of M'Langi tea.

His mother's tales had told of their early adventures, the two of them roaming the mountains on the uninhabited islands, in search of the special tree from whose bark and leaves the tea was made.

He'd been two years old when his father, working with a local friend, had been killed by a rockfall on an outer island.

Two years old when his mother and he had moved into the comfortable, self-contained annexe off the big Lockhart house. It was only after Caroline and Christopher were born, and their mother died, that old Mrs Lockhart had offered his mother a job—helping with the baby and generally running the house.

'I thought I might find you here.'

Caroline's voice startled him out of his reverie.

'What are you doing? What about your patients?'

'Hettie sent me home. Sam's just checked our patients and decided Mina can manage them.'

She sank down beside him on the grass.

'When I came back to work at the hospital,' he told her, 'I brought my mother's ashes here and scattered them in the grass.'

'So she and your father could be together.'

Caroline spoke quietly, a statement, not a question.

She rested her hand gently on his shoulder, and his skin burned beneath the touch, his body warring with his mind, wanting her so badly, yet here, beside his mother—

He *had* to tell Caro.

Now, before anything went any further…

But she was so damned insecure, wouldn't his marriage—for all it was over now—seem like a further betrayal?

Hurt her as much as his deserting her had?

She slid her hand down his arm to grasp his fingers.

'Come on,' she said, 'let's visit my mother now.'

They'd done this so often as children, coming to the little cemetery, sitting among the graves, talking to her mother and his father, telling them what they'd been doing, laughing, and sometimes crying.

They reached Charlotte Lockhart's memorial—a simple stone with her name and the words 'wife and mother'—Max having given the initial of her name to both her children.

'Hold me,' Caroline whispered, and Keanu put his arms around her and drew her close, feeling her softness, her breasts against his chest, long silky hair tickling his neck, covering his hands that now held her to him.

She raised her head, and he caught the glisten of tears in her eyes.

Her eyes were shadowed with memories, and not happy ones. This was Caro, so he kissed them, first one and then the other, his lips sliding to her temple, teeth nibbling at her ear lobe, kisses along her jaw, although her mouth—that wide, sensual mouth—had always been his destination.

Or so it seemed as he tasted her, his tongue sliding around her lips, delving, probing.

Had her mouth opened to him?

Were her lips responding?

For a moment it seemed as if she might have been a statue, then, with a groan that started somewhere down near her toes, she kissed him back, her mouth moving on his, her hands exploring his shoulders, arms, neck, gripping at his hair, his head, holding his mouth to hers as if her life depended on it.

They were in a graveyard.

His parents were here...

Somehow his lips had slipped lower, kissing her neck, while she pressed hers against his head and murmured his name. His hand had slid beneath her shirt, found a breast, a full breast that felt heavy in his hand. His thumb strayed across the nipple, already peaked by the heat of the kiss.

She'd dragged his head back to kiss his lips, so he gave in and let her, matched the heat of her kisses, and the little moan she gave as his fingers teased the taut nipple was like honey in his mouth.

Had his legs given way that he was on his knees, still holding Caroline, their bodies pressed together? Moonlight cast shadows from the trees around the graveyard, picked out writing on the stone beside which they knelt.

Charlotte Lockhart.

Wife and mother…

Wife!

'This is crazy,' he whispered as he eased himself away from Caroline, his body throbbing with need, hers hot within his hands, which had settled on her shoulders. 'I'm sorry, there's something I should have said—told you— have to tell you.'

Blue-green eyes—dazed with desire?—stared at him and she shook her head, as if trying to take in his stumbling words.

She released the grip she'd had on his shirt, raised her hands to lift his off her shoulders, then bowed her head so the hair on the top of her head brushed against his chest.

He saw her shoulders move as she took a deep breath, then she lifted her head and looked at him, into his eyes, hers questioning now but so beautiful.

Too beautiful to hurt?

Perhaps he could contact his lawyer first, before he told her, find out the situation…

Coward!

He took her hands in his and eased her back down onto the ground.

'So tell,' she said quietly.

But words wouldn't come. *I'm married* seemed too blunt, far too hurtful.

'It's about attraction,' he finally began. 'About attraction and love and how there can be one without the other but how do you know at the beginning?'

'Are you talking about our attraction?' she asked, her head turned not to him but towards the distant sea, so all he could see was her profile—no emotion...

'Not really but in a way, yes, and I should have told you earlier. I should have told you when it happened—but we'd been apart so long and I really didn't know how to. And I certainly should have told you before I kissed you.'

Now she turned to him.

'It's something bad, isn't it? You're already married, or engaged? I should have guessed. Why wouldn't you be?'

She went to rise, but he caught her hand and kept her on the grass beside him.

'Married but separated for five years,' he finally admitted. 'It was attraction, nothing more, but we didn't discover that until after we were married. We weren't exactly virgins, but Mum's greatest pain, later when she did eventually talk about Ian, was that she'd lost her moral compass—the ethical code by which she'd always lived. And that was in my mind—some half-formed ethical code that said if we were having sex we should get married. We'd met at uni, as physio and medical students—our paths crossed often—and the attraction was definitely there. Marriage seemed a great idea, but something didn't gel. We didn't fight, we didn't hurt each other, we just kind of drifted in different directions and in the end sat down and talked about it and agreed it had been a mistake.'

He ran out of words and leaned back on his elbows, looking up at the silvery moon above them.

'Where is she?' Caro asked.

He shrugged.

'She went to Melbourne. We didn't keep in touch, nor did we get around to divorcing. I don't know why—perhaps because it seemed like admitting what a huge mistake we'd made. Anyway, a couple of months ago she contacted me, told me she wanted a divorce and sent the papers.

She'd met someone else, sounded so happy I was pleased for her, so I signed the papers. They'll go before a judge some time soon, then a month and a day later I won't be married any more.'

Caroline had sat, stunned into silence, as Keanu told his tale. Somehow, in all her thoughts of Keanu over the years, the fact that he might marry had never occurred to her.

Not that it should matter, but obviously it did, because her heart was hurting, and her throat was tight, and what she really wanted to do was hit out at him.

But why shouldn't he have married?

Wouldn't she have married Steve if he hadn't dumped her when the mine had gone bad?

'Did you think of me at all?'

She wasn't sure where the question had come from, but heard it make its way out of her dry mouth.

'Only every minute of the ceremony, which is when I realised how wrong it all was. But I put that aside, and gave the marriage all I had, Caro. Moral compass stuff again. We were friends as well as lovers and I didn't want to hurt her.'

Now Caroline was sorry she'd asked the question, sorry about so much, but the pain in her heart remained and she knew she had to get away—think about this, work out why now, when it was all over, it was hurting her.

Why his being married was so ridiculously hurtful, especially as he wasn't really married at all…

And shouldn't he have told her all this before they'd kissed—the first time, not the last time?

Even if he wasn't *married* married, shouldn't it have been mentioned in passing?

She touched his shoulder as she stood up, then made her way up to the house, her mind so full of conjecture it felt too heavy for her neck.

* * *

Vaguely recalling, through a foggy haze of lust and shock, that Keanu had mentioned something about her being on duty at six, Caroline got herself out of bed, dressed, ate a lamington Bessie had apparently baked the previous day, drank a glass of milk and headed down to the hospital.

This time of the year, it was light by five in the morning, but half an hour later than that the morning still had a pearly glow and the sound of the birds waking up, the calm sea beyond the rainforest, and a sense of the world coming alive with a fresh new morning filled her with unexpected happiness.

True, there were problems but right now nothing, but nothing, seemed insurmountable.

Inevitably, Hettie was already there, in spite of Caroline being twenty minutes early.

'Anahera's off duty today and will be helping her mother with preparations for Alkiri's funeral. In fact, the fire's already been started in the fire pit.'

Fire? Fire pit?

The words seemed hard to understand in a hospital, until Carolyn remembered where she was and what was happening today—a funeral and funeral feast.

'Keanu's also gone down to the research station to help set everything up,' Hettie added. 'I'll take a look at the young lad with the ulcer before I hand over. I don't think the medication is working. I'll talk to Sam about changing the combination, but watch him carefully and if there's any sign of fever get Sam or Keanu here immediately.'

The diabetic patient was up and dressed.

'Doesn't want to miss the funeral feast,' Hettie said dryly. 'I'll sign her out later.'

She turned to Caroline.

'Okay, so you'll only have one patient, but that's largely

because everyone knows we're short-staffed and puts off coming to see us, either here or at the island clinics. But our one patient needs all the care we can give him, never forget that, and if you don't get one or two coming up from the feast with burnt toes or cut fingers I'd be very surprised. Apparently, the festivities kick off at ten—well, the funeral part, anyway.'

She paused, then added, 'I understand Alkiri was a friend of yours and you'd really like to be there, but the foreman wants to show Sam and me the laboratories— showing off, I suppose—and Keanu's doing the oration so he has to be there. Our second aide will be here with you. Her shift doesn't begin until eight, but if there's any problem at all, phone me or Sam—our cell numbers are by the phone in the main office.'

Caroline took it all in, and much as her heart longed to be there to say goodbye to Alkiri, she knew being left here was a sign of her acceptance. Lockhart or not, Hettie was trusting her.

What Caroline hadn't realised was that the statement— 'Anahera is helping her mother with the celebration feast'— meant Vailea was not in the kitchen. Apparently, nurses here made and served breakfast to their patients when called upon to do so.

Vailea—bless her heart, or perhaps her organisational skills—had a list of all meals up on a corkboard near the door. Not only were the meal menus there, but they had the requisite 'GF' for gluten free, and a little heart beside ones suggested for heart patients.

Back to her patients—checking their notes: no dietary restrictions for either of them.

According to—

'How are you doing?'

Keanu was there, right behind her.

'I thought you were busy with the *hangi*,' she said, needing to say something as an almost overwhelming rush of what could only be lust weakened her knees.

She was *still* feeling that lust thing?

He was married!

And he hadn't told her.

Anyway, might he not be right about the dangers of attraction, which was just a weaker word for lust?

And shouldn't she show *some* reaction to this information?

But what?

'Too many cooks,' he said lightly, and she had to grapple her way back through her thoughts to where the conversation had started. 'I'm not needed until a lot later. I'm doing the oration.'

The lightness vanished from his voice with the last sentence, and yet again Caroline's first instinct was to hug him.

But hugs led to—

Well, trouble.

Change the subject.

'You've been down to check? They've got the fire going?'

He nodded, so close now she could see the smooth golden skin of his face—the strong chin he must have shaved extra-carefully this morning.

And being that close, *he* must be able to see she was having difficulty breathing.

She ducked behind a table, and he stood opposite her.

'And?'

'The women are hanging flower leis and putting huge baskets of leaves all around the place. It's really beautiful, Caro.'

'Sounds lovely but I've got to get breakfasts,' she managed, although her mind was on the kiss they'd shared the previous evening, not bacon and eggs.

'I know,' he said, his voice husky, his eyes unreadable.

'I really wanted to tell you I went down to see Reuben this morning just to confirm the order to close the mine.'

The broad shoulders that had felt so solid beneath her hands lifted in a shrug.

'I said it was a health and safety issue and, as a doctor overseeing that, I had the authority to issue the shutdown notice.'

Caroline sighed.

'That was silly. You've put yourself into the firing line of the workers' anger now. They already hate the Lockhart name, so what harm could a little more hate do? And as it's Ian's fault that the mine's in the state it's in, it's a Lockhart issue anyway.'

Keanu's sigh was almost as deep as her own.

'We'll just have to wait and see,' he said quietly. 'Reuben's going to get someone in from Atangi to fence the site and he was going to tell the small crew still working as soon as I was out of sight.'

'So they wouldn't rend you limb from limb?' Caroline queried, although she couldn't find even the slightest of smiles to go with the suggestion.

'Probably,' Keanu agreed. 'But it's done now, so that's one less thing for you to worry about. Let's get started on these breakfasts.'

He'd done it so she could stop worrying about it?

'Weren't you talking about making breakfasts?'

One word, and a practical one at that, yet tingles still ran down her spine.

'Of course. I've only got two and shortly I'll be down to one patient, but would you mind asking them what they fancy for breakfast? Vailea's left a list—there's scrambled, boiled or fried eggs, bacon, baked beans, toast and jam, and I think there's cereal.'

'I might have to have the lot to wake me up,' he said before turning and walking out of the kitchen.

To wake him up?

It hadn't been *that* late when they'd parted.

So, had he, like she, lain awake long into the night, re-thinking the kiss?

Or had he been thinking about his marriage?

About his wife?

Though perhaps he'd been worried about the mine closure and his decision to be the one to tell Reuben? Kept awake by things that had nothing at all to do with the heated, almost desperate kiss and the discussion that had followed it.

CHAPTER NINE

FINDING THE RATHER large kitchen altogether too small to share with Caro, Keanu delivered the breakfast orders and departed, excusing himself by explaining he wanted to change the dressings on the Buruli ulcer, which was causing both him and Sam a lot of concern.

It wasn't responding to the medication, the young lad was in severe pain and the flesh was continuing to deteriorate, as was the lad's general condition.

'Are you sure nothing got into it before you came in here?' he asked as he deadened the area around the wound to clean it yet again.

'Could have.' A shrug strengthened the typical boy reply.

'Like what?' Keanu asked, but all he got that time was a shake of his head.

He put the new dressing on the wound, wrote up stronger painkillers and was departing when the young aide, having just started on duty, brought in the breakfast tray.

Time he was gone, yet his feet led him to the kitchen.

'Hettie tells me she'll be here just before ten so you can come down to the longhouse.'

All he got for a reply was a frown, although eventually she must have summoned up enough courage to speak.

'I—um—I'm not sure, Keanu. I really don't like funerals—even the island celebratory ones. I hate that people say all the nice things about someone after they're dead and can't hear them. Why don't people tell them that stuff before they die?'

Keanu moved across the kitchen towards her and put his arms around her.

'You did tell him, Caroline, when we sat with him before he died. He knew how much he meant to you and if you don't want to come down, of course you shouldn't. I guess Hettie just assumed you would want to.'

He felt her body rest against his and tension drain from it. He longed to kiss her, but now he knew where kisses led…

He shouldn't have come close enough to touch her, let alone give her a hug, at least until they'd had time to talk about last night's revelations. About how she felt, about whether it mattered at the moment that he was still married…

So he let his lips brush the soft, golden hair on the top of her head and eased away from her.

'I'll bring you some food later,' he said, and got out of the place before the regret that he *hadn't* kissed her overcame his common sense.

The longhouse was busier than he'd expected, and he could pick out people from every inhabited island in the group. The harbour down at the mine would be crowded with boats and the old truck would have been ferrying locals from there to the research station all morning.

Someone had put a row of chairs at one end of the building, and he and the elders took their places there. The crowd grew quiet when he spoke, talking with love of the man he'd known—the young, strong man who'd been a master

boatman, often called upon to rescue people who had fool-
ishly put out to sea when the weather was bad.

He reminded his people of some of the history of
M'Langi that Alkiri had passed on to him, true tales and
folklore, fascinating stories for two story-hungry young-
sters.

And finally he asked for others to speak, and speak
they did. A flood of reminiscences followed, first the elders, then ordinary people whose lives Alkiri had touched.

Swallowing a lump of emotion as he listened, he was
almost glad Caro wasn't here. Always a softie, she'd have
been in floods of tears by now.

Caro…

A disturbance of some kind at the back of the longhouse
brought him out of his reverie—useless reverie, in fact.

There were raised voices, angry voices, then one of the
men departed, maybe told to leave by someone senior to
them.

But the bits and pieces of talk he'd heard suggested the
man was going to the hospital. He could see Hettie and
Sam sitting with the works foreman, Hettie having obviously returned when Caroline had explained she wasn't
coming down.

Caroline!

The man was a miner…

With a very hasty excuse to the nearest elder he departed, following the man up the hill, hurrying to catch
up, to get in front of him.

He recognised him.

Definitely one of the miners he'd seen the other day.

He called to him but in spite of the early hour the man
had probably been drinking and nothing could make him
deviate from his determined path.

Keanu was close on the miner's heels when he reached

the gate near the airstrip and there Keanu diverted from the miner's path, taking the back way, which he knew was shorter, running now, his heart thudding in his chest, reaching the hospital and racing in, calling for Caro.

He must have looked and sounded like a madman because she reached out her hand and rested it on his arm.

'Calm down, Keanu, tell me what's up.'

'Go back to the house—no, he'll go there next. Go out the back. My villa is the lowest one. Go inside and lock the door.'

He could hear the man by now, ranting about the closure, and knew how close he must be.

'Go now,' he said to her, but she stood her ground, wanting an explanation.

The phone broke their stalemate and she answered it, turning back to him to say, 'That was Hettie to tell you Sam and some of the young men are on their way. On their way where? What's happening?'

But it was too late for explanations. The angry man was already on the hospital steps, his voice crying out for a Lockhart and, woman or not, any Lockhart would do.

'I can't have them coming in here—there are patients, well, one patient. I'll go out and see him.'

Keanu grabbed her shoulders as she started to move past him, pulling her back, thrusting her towards the kitchen.

'At least go in there and lock the door. *I'll* talk to him!'

He turned away, sure the man wouldn't hurt a woman, yet only half sure. Who knew what a man made brave by cava might do?

'She's not here,' he said, meeting the man on the veranda. 'And she's not up at the house so don't bother looking there. Anyway, I'm the one who closed the mine, and it was for the safety of all the miners. It's a temporary measure until we find some money to give everyone their back-pay and start things up again.'

'That's what you say, Keanu, but for all your closeness you're not a Lockhart and we all know what *they* can do.'

The man pushed forward, but Keanu blocked the doorway.

'This is a hospital, not a boxing ring,' he reminded them. 'Let's talk about this in the garden.'

No one moved—well, the man threw a punch, which missed Keanu's jaw by a whisker but still served to fire his anger.

He hit back, knocking the culprit down the steps.

It had been stupid. He knew that immediately, because now he'd made the man look foolish, and that had angered him even more. He righted himself and pressed forward again and this time the punch that was thrown connected, knocking Keanu sideways against the door-jamb. He'd barely straightened when he felt a shove from behind, and Caroline stood there, hands on her hips and fury in her eyes.

'That's enough!' she said. 'Keanu's right, this is a hospital. And you are right as well—it *was* a Lockhart who brought the troubles on you. But he was one bad apple. Do you think I'm not as upset as you all are?'

The answer was another roar of anger. Keanu spun Caroline behind him.

'Go and protect the patients—lock the ward doors if you can, or put furniture against them.'

Would she do it?

No time to find out but somehow he had to protect her.

'Caroline's right about the one bad apple,' he said to the man who still loomed on the steps. 'But he's gone now and I know the Lockharts are doing all they can to fix things, Caroline in particular.'

'The mine's closed—what can *she* do?'

'Find the money to get the mine started again, to pay the wages you're all owed. But in the meantime, think of the other things the Lockhart family has done for you—and will continue to do in the future. You've got kids. If you chase them off, and the hospital closes, where do you go when one of your kids is stung by a stonefish? And what job will you have if you don't allow us time to get the mine operating again?'

It had certainly quietened him down.

'Now move away, we don't want trouble here.'

The new voice made them turn. Sam was there and with him a group of elders and young men, very strong young men.

'Shame on you,' the senior of the elders said. 'You do something like this on a day when one of our most revered friends is being laid to rest. And now the feast is ready— let us celebrate his life.'

The fight seemed to ooze out of the man, although Keanu wondered if he might return.

Or worse, raid the house while Caroline slept inside it…

CHAPTER TEN

SAM RETURNED TO the celebration. As guest of the resort foreman he had to stay for the feast, but Hettie insisted on remaining at the hospital.

'You go down,' she said to Caroline, who shook her head.

'Go down there where people hate the very mention of my name? I know that lout was drunk, but he was probably expressing the sentiments of most of the community. I doubt if anything will ever restore our name, given the amount of damage Ian's done—and I only know little scraps of it.'

'Something will work out,' Hettie said, but with so little conviction Caroline knew she was only being kind.

She probably didn't think much of the Lockhart family herself.

And who could blame her?

'Then I'll just head up to the house,' she said to Hettie, thinking she'd phone her father just to talk to him, to ask about Christopher, then...

Get back to the books.

'You will not go up to the house,' Hettie said firmly. 'Not until Keanu, or Jack or Sam are here to go with you, and then only to get whatever you need, then you can come back down here and stay in one of the empty nurses' villas.'

It bothered Caroline that even Hettie was being protective. Surely there wasn't that much risk.

Well, she could forget the phone call, but she had to do something.

And surely all this fuss was overdone...

Hettie had disappeared so Caroline slipped out of the hospital, taking the back path up to the house in case the angry man was still lurking around. It took her only minutes to collect what she wanted, then she headed back down the track, not to one of the nurses' villas but to Keanu's place.

Somehow she knew she'd be safe in Keanu's place.

The door was unlocked and as she entered and looked around, she had to smile. Helen had insisted they both keep their rooms neat and tidy and it was obvious the rule had stuck with Keanu for longer than it had stuck with her.

The little place was neat and functional. The design offered a largish room with a sitting space, a dining space and beyond that the kitchen. Off that, to the right, was the bedroom, complete with double bed—did married couples often choose to work here?

She smiled to herself at the naivety of the thought. Of course there were likely to be relationships among staff working in such an isolated place. Wasn't Jack hoping to win over the beautiful Anahera?

But going into Keanu's bedroom and what was presumably a bathroom off it was a step too far, so she dumped the little notebook and laptop on the dining table.

And sat down to do some work.

She still didn't have the running costs of the mine but Reuben would know, or once she found Peter she could get a rough figure from him. Where they'd get the money she didn't have a clue, but somehow she had to do this. She made up neat lists. The back pay she could put a figure against but superannuation had a question mark, as had running costs. And she'd have to work out how much pay was owed to Bessie and Harold.

On top of that, if she was going to continue to live at the house, she should check what food was there. The next flight was Friday—she should order supplies...

As she paused, considering what to do next, she heard the music from the longhouse. It flowed through her blood and sent her fingers tapping until she stood up and began to move. She would never have the lithe grace of the island-ers but she couldn't help swaying her hips to the rhythm of the music.

Keanu had teased her...

Had she summoned him up by thought wave that he appeared in the doorway? She stopped her movement im-mediately before he teased her again.

'Don't tell me you've actually done what you were told,' he said, then he looked at the book and laptop on the table. 'Well, not entirely, you obviously went up to the house to get those and I'll bet no one went with you.'

'Everyone's back at the party—I was quite safe,' she retorted, then sniffed the air and looked at the basket he carried in one hand.

'You've brought food? Oh, Keanu, thank you. It is so long since I tasted *hangi* meat and vegetables.'

She pushed the laptop to one end of the small table and hurried into the kitchen area, finding plates on her second foray into the cupboards and cutlery in the top drawer she expected it to be in.

Keanu had taken a cloth off the top of the delicacies in the basket and the aromas made Caroline's mouth water.

He divided the food onto the two plates, stopping when she protested it was too much. But the delicious, tender pork, the taro and potatoes disappeared from her plate in no time, conversation forgotten as the food took them back to happier times when they'd often attended island feasts.

'Were you dancing as I came in?' Keanu asked when she'd pushed her plate away unfinished, and he'd slowed down his eating enough to talk.

'Maybe moving just a little,' she admitted. 'As you've told me so many times, girls with European blood can't dance.'

He smiled, remembering, as she had been, and sadness for those lost days filled her soul.

Keanu read the sadness in her eyes and knew what she was thinking.

'Our childhood was truly blessed,' he said quietly.

He set down his knife and fork and pushed his plate away, but as Caroline stood up to take it, he reached out and took her hand, closing his fingers around hers.

Just that touch sent messages he didn't want to acknowledge streaming through his body, but he needed to say what he had to say.

'I want you to stay here tonight, Caro. The rabble-rousers—if it turns out to be more than one—will probably be too drunk to do anything other than sleep but in case they want more trouble, they certainly won't go door to door in the hospital quarters in search of you.'

She eased her hand out of his and stepped back.

'No way. They could attack the house,' she reminded him. 'Not find me there, and become angry, burn the place. I can't stay here, Keanu. I'll get Bessie and Harold to stay there with me if you really believe there's any danger.'

She hesitated, and he sensed she wanted to say more.

But she returned to gathering up the dishes, taking them to the kitchen, putting leftover food into the refrigerator—busywork while she avoided him in case he asked what was going on.

'Aren't you in charge over at the hospital?' she asked when she'd finished cleaning. 'If you don't mind, I'll stay here until the party is over, then track down Bessie and Harold to ask them about tonight.'

Bessie and Harold, both well into their sixties, would be fine protection. He supposed if she was insistent about staying in the house, he'd have to stay there too, which, in fact, would be preferable to both of them staying here, her in the bed—he'd insist on that—and him on the couch, aware in every fibre of his being that she was there, so close.

And how could he return to that bed when she'd departed?

Wouldn't he always feel her presence there? Smell the Caro scent of her on the sheets and pillowslip?

'I'll be over at the hospital,' he said, knowing he had to get away from her before he was completely tied in knots. 'Hettie's very worried about the ulcer—worrying if we've misdiagnosed it as it seems to be getting worse, not better. You call when you're going up to the house and I'll walk you up.'

For a moment he thought she'd argue, but instead she flipped him a snappy salute, said, 'Yes, sir!' and opened her notebook again.

She wasn't going to stop Keanu sleeping in the house—Caroline was only too aware of his stubbornness—but it would be better than having him sleeping in the big house somewhere far from her, rather than right next door, through partition walls that wouldn't hold back the essence of him that seemed to fill her whenever he was near.

Every time she closed her eyes she felt the kiss they'd shared in the graveyard—felt the longing in her body for them to have taken it further.

But wasn't it too soon?

Of course it was.

And he was married.

Her senseless mental meandering led nowhere so she

sighed, gathered up the books and was halfway up the hill before she remembered she was supposed to summon Keanu to guard her on her walk.

But Bessie and Harold were there, arguing on the track not far from her, so she was safe.

'We are staying at your place tonight and don't you argue, missy.'

She'd caught up with Bessie and Harold, and on this subject they were obviously united for Bessie spoke and Harold nodded his head very firmly.

Harold and Bessie she could handle in the house.

But Keanu?

He came at nine.

Bessie had made a salad to go with leftover pork from the feast, and she, Harold and Caroline had eaten it at the kitchen table, Bessie refusing to eat in the dining room.

'Makes me too sad to see that lovely chandelier and think of your grandma polishing each crystal,' she said, by way of explanation. And in truth Caroline felt much the same way—plus she still had papers spread across the table, and although it looked like a mess, she knew where to put her hand on every record there.

She was sitting on the swing seat on the front veranda, watching the last flights of the seabirds—dark whirling shadows against the early evening sky, returning to their roosts on the island.

They were a fairly good reflection of her thoughts at the moment—dark and whirling.

The cause of her distraction appeared on the track below the house, striding resolutely up from the hospital accommodation, clad now in linen shorts and a dark green T-shirt—a man at home in his environment.

And wasn't she at home in hers?

Of course she was and the shiver of whatever it was

that had coursed through her body was probably only relief at seeing him.

Except that she hadn't been frightened by the loud voice and accusations earlier and she was reasonably sure that man and all the others would have drunk themselves stupid and collapsed into bed by now.

'Evening,' he said, touching a forefinger to an imaginary hat.

'And good evening to you,' Caroline replied. She could do this—she really could. All she had to do was completely divorce herself from all the manifestations of attraction that the wretched man was causing in her body.

But when he sat down beside her on the swing, took her hand and began to push the swing gently back and forth with his foot, she lost what little resolve she'd managed to gather, rested her head on his shoulder and swung with him, just as they had so many times in the past.

The moon rose majestically from the water, the birds had quietened and a peace she hadn't felt for a long time spread through her veins.

So even when Keanu turned to press a light kiss on her shoulder she barely reacted.

That was if you could define a small electric shock as barely…

'Nice here, isn't it?' he said, and although she'd swear neither of them had moved, their bodies were now touching from shoulder to hip and their clasped hands were in Keanu's lap.

Worse was the cloud that had wrapped around them, some unseen yet almost tangible blanket of desire.

Or maybe he couldn't feel it.

Maybe it was just her.

Being silly.

Imagining things.

'Not going away, is it, this attraction?' he said quietly, and she knew it wasn't imagination.

'Not really,' she answered, although the truth would have been *not at all*.

He turned away from a fascination with the moon to look directly at her.

'So, how do we tell?'

'If it's love?' she asked, guessing his earlier experience of attraction had made it hard to use the word. 'I wonder...'

Although maybe she *knew*.

Didn't her heart beating faster when she caught a glimpse of him, or heard his voice or even thought of him suggest it had to be love?

Was lying sleepless in her bed, her body wired, wanting...?

Him!

Was that love?

Or was it old friendship mixed up with attraction?

For a long time he didn't speak, and she wondered if he'd been giving it the same thought she had but had come to a different conclusion.

'So much has happened between us,' he said quietly. 'I let you down once before, Caroline, and please believe me when I say that it hurt me too. Then marrying. Not telling you. I let you down again. But now—now I'd cut off my hand if it would help you to forgive me.'

Her heart was juddering in her chest, the beat every which way, while some kind of madness filled her mind—a madness begging her to take him to her bed, to rip off all his clothes and dispense with the agony that was attraction.

With Harold and Bessie here?

So lighten up!

'And what would I do with a bloody hand?' she teased, and though he laughed, she hadn't quite achieved her aim for he'd let go of her hand and wrapped his arm around her shoulders, drawing her closer, close enough to look into her eyes and probably see through them to the muddle in her head.

The kiss, when it inevitably came, was like nothing she'd experienced before. A barely there brush of lips on lips, then butterfly kisses across her cheeks, her eyelids and her temple.

With maddening deliberation, his mouth eventually returned to hers, but only to tease again, his teeth nibbling softly at her lips, tongue darting in to touch her tongue, withdrawing, darting, departing so her lips were hot then cool, and the pressure building within her was volcanic— a volcano about to blow.

He must have kicked with his foot, for the swing began to move again, and the movement lulled her senses, so when his tongue invaded her mouth and his hand brushed against her breast, she sighed and leaned into him, welcoming him, kissing him back, the intensity of the kiss growing until it blotted out her mind.

It was such a cliché, sitting on a porch swing, kissing like this.

Keanu was desperately trying to keep a grasp on reality, to keep his mind from going blank and letting his body take over all his actions.

They'd stop soon—well, they could hardly make love out here, especially not when there might be murderous miners wandering around.

But right now kissing Caroline was filling his soul with delight. His body wasn't quite so delighted, wanting more than fervid kisses.

Did he love her?

Her tongue was tangling with his, and he felt almost painfully aroused, but he couldn't break the kiss, couldn't pull his lips from hers, his arms from around her body.

She was his.

That was what the kiss was saying.

His kiss, and her response, making a statement.

About the future?

Or about attraction?

'Go to bed,' he whispered, his lips close to her ear. 'Maddie is back tomorrow, and a FIFO nurse is joining her, so we'll both have time off. We'll talk.'

'About?' she murmured back.

'About us, and our future, and attraction and love and all kinds of things.'

She smiled and kissed him gently on the lips, her eyes bright with unshed tears.

Tears of happiness this time, the brilliance of her smile told him that.

He stood up and pulled her upright, then turned her and nudged her towards the front door.

'I'll sleep on the couch out here. Reuben's got some sensible young men staked out around the veranda, and Harold's in a swag in the kitchen.'

He knew she was going to protest, so he kissed her again—swift and hard—then pulled back.

'Go,' he said.

CHAPTER ELEVEN

KEANU WAS DOWN at the hospital early—just the thought of Caroline asleep inside the house had been enough to keep him sleepless. Deciding to use the time productively, he stopped in at the office, realising it had been a couple of days since he'd dealt with his emails. He logged on to the computer and drummed his fingers as he waited for the screen to load.

And suddenly, there it was. An email from his solicitor in Cairns. So it was official—just like that, and without a word exchanged between him and his ex, his marriage was dissolved. He was a free man, although in truth he'd never been free. Not from the only person who'd ever held his heart. Just what did this mean for him and Caroline? In so many ways this wasn't the right time, but if not now, then when? If she could forgive him, then maybe, just maybe, she could love him.

But Keanu was roused from his musings by the sudden appearance of Sam in the office.

'Keanu, I'm glad you're here. I've just been looking at that ulcer again. The more I see it, the more convinced I am that we're dealing with something different here. I'd value a second opinion.'

Forcing his thoughts back to his work, Keanu nodded briskly. 'Of course. I agree that there's more to this than meets the eye. Has our patient said anything else about it to you?'

Sam shook his head as he pushed open the door to the ward, Keanu following right behind. They made their way to Raoul's bedside, where Keanu leant over to examine the uncovered wound.

'It's not looking good,' Keanu agreed, frowning in concentration.

'Not only that, but according to the limited testing I've been able to do, and our patient's response to the medication—or total lack of response—it just has to be something else, but I've no idea what eats away at the flesh so badly and just continues to degrade the wound.'

'Hydrofluoric acid.'

Keanu wasn't sure where the answer had come from, though apparently it had surfaced from some deep recess in his mind.

Which must have been working, for all he felt like a very confused zombie what with all that was happening in his personal life right now...

Sam turned to face him, grabbed his arm and steered him back out through the door.

'What did you say?'

'Hydrofluoric acid,' Keanu repeated, but with more certainty this time. 'Dreadful stuff. It just eats away at the skin and flesh and if you happen to drink it you're done for.'

'Well, I'm glad you kept that little bit of information to yourself until we were away from the patient. I don't think I've ever heard of it—though I probably did as a student—but I've never come across it as an acid burn. Except...' He paused in thought. 'Now I look at the wound as an acid burn it's starting to make sense. But this—what did you call it?'

'Hydrofluoric acid. It's the only acid that eats through glass so has to be kept in plastic containers. Years ago a very small concentration of it was used in a product for taking rust marks out of clothing but I think that's been banned now.'

'So why on earth would anyone have any of it on the fairly isolated islands of M'Langi? If it's as dangerous as you say, you can't just order a gallon or two off the internet.'

'I doubt a plane would carry it. But someone's brought it back here in hand luggage or by boat. Apparently there *are* places you can buy it. I imagine it has commercial uses of some kind or it wouldn't still be manufactured.'

Sam frowned at him.

'But why?'

Keanu heard the plane coming in, hopefully bringing relief staff, but Sam showed no desire to go rushing off to meet it.

'Keanu?'

Neither would he until he got an answer.

'It dissolves glass,' he repeated. 'And glass is made of sand, which is very degraded quartz, and gold comes in quartz veins. You pop a piece of gold-bearing quartz into a jar of hydrofluoric and, *voilà*, in a couple of days you have wee nuggets of gold.'

Sam was staring at him in disbelief.

'You're saying men steal gold-bearing quartz from the mine?'

He hadn't really been saying that—hadn't wanted to mention the matter at all—but they had a patient...

'Not all of them, and I'd say theft was rare back when the place was properly managed, but those who haven't been paid for a while probably feel they deserve it. Some of them might pinch it anyway—no one's perfect.'

He certainly had Sam's attention now.

'So, it's possible our patient had been fooling around with probably his father's acid and splashed some on his skin. Wouldn't he know?'

Keanu shook his head.

'Maybe not straight away, and when it started to hurt—from all accounts it's extremely painful—he didn't want to tell anyone about it because I'm sure he'd been forbidden to go near it, let alone open the lid of the container. Sniffing the fumes in close quarters can do horrible things to your lungs. No, he was hardly likely to tell his family what he'd done.'

'Treatment?'

Again Keanu could only shake his head.

'I was a child when I heard about it and even if the treatment was discussed it would have gone over my head. Best you get onto the internet or call the poisons centre back in Oz.'

Sam sighed, but before he could say anything a gorgeous and very pregnant young woman with short auburn curls, startling green eyes and a smile that lit up the air around her swept into the hospital.

'Maddie!' he and Sam cried in unison, holding out their arms and somehow gathering her in a three-way hug.

Which was when Caroline walked in.

Now was not the time to fill Caro in on his divorce; instead, Keanu made the introductions.

'Maddie, this is Caroline Lockhart. She filled in for us this week when the FIFO nurse didn't come.'

'And has been doing a great job,' Sam added.

He'd interrupted Keanu's, 'Caroline, this is Maddie Haddon, one of our favourite FIFO doctors.'

'Your only FIFO doctor now you've decided you'll be permanent, Keanu,' Maddie corrected as she held out her hand towards Caroline.

The introduction was interrupted as Bugsy, obviously hearing his mistress's voice, came hurtling towards her.

Maddie crouched awkwardly to hug her ecstatic dog.

'So much for my walking him twice a day,' Sam complained, 'but now you're here, Maddie, do you know anything about hydrofluoric acid?'

Maddie looked a little startled but she accepted Sam's hand to help her upright again, and shrugged her shoulders.

'That's the stuff that melts glass so has to be kept in plastic containers,' she offered.

'I think we've already established that. Come through to the office and you can tell me all your news—check-up okay?—while I look up how to treat a hydrofluoric burn.'

They disappeared along the corridor, and Caroline followed Keanu into the young lad's room. He could feel her closeness—aware of her in a way he'd never been before.

'You think it's an acid burn?' she asked him, all business.

Keanu wasn't sure what to feel. Last night they'd sat together and talked of love and attraction, and his body clamoured to greet her with a kiss—at least a kiss...

But work was work.

Caroline was by the patient's bed, leaning forward to examine the wound, so Keanu joined her, pushing the swirl of emotions inside him out of his mind with the practicalities of work.

He bent over Raoul and spoke quietly to him.

'Did you spill something on your leg?'

The slightest of head movements, but definitely a very subdued yes.

'Can you tell me what it was?'

Another shake of the head, this one just as definitely negative.

'You're not going to get into trouble,' Keanu said gently, 'at least not from us, but we do need to know so we can treat it before it gets any worse.'

How he was enduring the pain now, Keanu didn't know, having heard horror stories of hydrofluoric burns.

'Calcium glucanate gel,' Sam announced, coming in to join them by the bed. 'We don't have it but I can make it up. In the meantime, Caroline, would you take a blood sample so can we check if it's affected his electrolytes and, Keanu, can you flush the wound again to remove the cream we've been using?'

He turned to Raoul.

'If you'd told us—' he began, but Keanu held up his hand.

'We've had that conversation and he's very sorry.'

Sam nodded and disappeared again, no doubt to mix the solution he needed.

Caroline tightened a ligature around Raoul's upper arm then tapped a vein inside his elbow. She was so aware of Keanu's presence she could feel her skin growing hot and tight.

While Keanu was doing nothing more than flush a wound?

Concentrating, remembering all her training, she slid the needle into the vein, released the ligature and drew out blood for testing, telling herself all the time that a strange conversation during one night on a swing didn't mean anything.

Or did it?

He said they'd talk.

She asked Raoul to hold the cotton-wool ball to the tiny wound while she set aside the phial and found some tape.

Professional, she could do it, for all her nerves were skittering with the…promise, maybe, that had been last night.

Pleased to escape Keanu's presence, she took the blood through to Sam.

'And?' Maddie prompted.

Caroline wondered if she looked as puzzled as she felt. 'And what?'

Maddie smiled at her.

'Just because I've been off the island doesn't mean I haven't been keeping up with the gossip. And that tells me that you and Keanu have renewed your old childhood friendship, though possibly the word *friendship* isn't quite enough to describe your relationship.'

'For heaven's sake, we've barely spent ten hours alone with each other and the gossip mill has us...'

She didn't have the words she needed.

'Practically married?' Maddie kindly put in.

Caroline sighed. Well, Keanu was married, just to somebody else, so no matter what island gossip suggested a real marriage between herself and Keanu wasn't even an outside possibility for the near future.

'Things haven't got quite that far,' she muttered, unwilling to share more with a virtual stranger.

'Well, there's still time,' Maddie said. 'Now, didn't Sam say you could take a break? Go home.'

Home.

The island *was* home to her and she'd been so happy here since her return. Disturbed by the problems, of course, and confused by her attraction to Keanu, but none of that had spoiled the feeling that she was back where she belonged.

Home.

Keanu.

What was *he* thinking?

Caroline sighed and headed up to the house, using the track past the lagoon, thinking a swim might clear her head.

But up at the house the bookwork beckoned. She hadn't got the maintenance and other day-to-day working figures of the mine from Reuben. Hoping he'd still be in the office there, organising the fencing off of the mine, she headed down the steep steps once again.

Keeping busy to keep her mind off Keanu.

But he was already there, sitting with Reuben in the shed.

Why wouldn't he be?

No reason, but something about the way the pair of them looked at her made her feel uneasy.

Keanu was the first to speak.

'We're just sorting out something here, Caro,' he said, and for some reason his voice sounded tight.

As if they'd been discussing her?

Of course they wouldn't have been…

'I'll see you later at the house,' he added, and knowing a dismissal when she heard it, she turned and headed back up the steps.

But halfway up she saw the faint marking of an old track, grassy now, and grown over with enthusiastic tropical vines and plants.

Had she been thinking of the grotto that she noticed it?

She certainly hadn't the last time she'd climbed the steps.

But her feet were already on the barely there track, picking their way through the tangled regrowth, quickening her pace where the track was clear but taking her time to find a way around where thorn bushes formed a barrier.

Hot and sticky, not to mention covered in burrs, she finally reached the pool where the water cascading down from the lagoon came to rest before trickling on past the village to the sea.

She breathed in the humid air, catching scents she couldn't quite identify, resting for a moment before turning towards the waterfall.

'You're being silly,' she told herself, speaking the words aloud in the hope they might stop this trek back into the past.

Didn't work, and she kept going, arriving eventually at the hidden space behind the waterfall, the water making music all around her, the thick fern growth giving the space a special magic.

He'd married someone else.

She told herself this was okay, only to be expected—of course he would have married, and it was only the small child she'd once been that was bleating *But he's mine* deep inside her head.

She sat on a rock, her clothes damp from spray, and tried to make sense of her life as it was—not as she'd once imagined it would be.

'Caro, are you in there?'

Keanu's voice.

How had he guessed?

And of course it wasn't anything to do with linked thoughts.

'Caro,' he called again, and this time she knew she'd have to answer.

'I'm in the grotto,' she called, and within minutes he was there beside her, sitting on what had always been 'his' rock.

'How did you know?' she asked.

'It was obvious that someone had been along the old track and as you were the only one stupid enough to be coming down here on your own, I just followed your trail.'

'Stupid enough?' she demanded, angry but not sure whether it was because her thinking time had been interrupted or because his presence always caused her tension.

'There could have been a landslip or a bit of the track washed away.'

'Well, there wasn't, and I'm quite safe, so you can go off and do whatever you were planning to do with Reuben.'

'Which was to come and see you,' Keanu told her, not as excited now as he'd been earlier, not quite as sure she was going to like the idea. And he'd already decided that now was not the time to mention his divorce. Other matters were more urgent after all.

'I was talking to Reuben about the mine. I talked to the elders about it yesterday, and spoke to your father this morning. Something you'd said about finding someone to invest in it—once we knew how much we needed—sparked a kind of shadow of an idea in my head, and it wasn't until yesterday at the funeral that I worked out what it was.'

He paused, waiting for a comment, perhaps a little excitement, or even a cool 'And?'

But there was no response so, feeling even more uncertain, he ploughed on.

'Reuben isn't the only islander with a son making good money on the mainland, so it seemed to me that the islanders themselves might like to invest in the mine, form a company of some sort, a co-op perhaps—and take it over.'

'Take it over?'

Caro's voice was scratchy.

'Completely?'

'That's why I had to talk to Max. I knew he'd know which way to go, the company or whatever, and of course he'd have to agree to the idea.'

'And he did? He's happy for the islanders to take over the mine?'

Keanu was worried now. He'd really expected excitement that he'd sorted out the problem, perhaps a little hesitation as Caro considered it. But not this flat, unemotional questioning.

Unable to work it out, he went with answering.

'Yes, of course. He was annoyed he hadn't thought of it himself. Of course, it can't happen overnight, but within maybe six months we could have the mine up and running again and money going into the hospital—that would still be part of the arrangement—with the shareholders benefiting as well.'

'And you never thought to talk to me about this?'

Not flat and unemotional now—no, now she was upset, although he couldn't fathom why.

'There's been no time,' he said, hoping to sooth whatever was bothering her. 'As you can imagine there's still so much to do. It's mainly been just contacting people.'

It was hard to see her expression in the gloom, but he saw the way she stood up, and knew from the way she held her body that she'd be glaring down at him.

'Contacting everyone but me!' she said. 'Do I not count? Wasn't I part of this save-the-mine project from the beginning? Wasn't I the one who got the books and put the figures together? Then suddenly it's all "Don't worry your little head about it, the men will fix it" and you don't even mention it to me?'

He stood too, and put a hand on her shoulder—a hand that was quickly shrugged off.

'Caro—' he began.

But she was already walking away, pausing only to say, 'You could have mentioned it as we sat on the swing, as we talked about love and what love was. I thought it was sharing, doing things together—not everything, that would be silly—but this was a joint project at the beginning, then suddenly it was all yours. I don't know how to feel, Keanu. I don't even know why I feel the way I do, when obviously it's the ideal solution for the mine, but right now I just have to get away by myself and try to work out what I really want from love.'

And with that she disappeared from the grotto, not going back along the track but climbing the rocks at the side of the waterfall.

She was as sure-footed as a cat, so he didn't worry about her going that way, and he knew it would be pointless trying to argue with her in the mood she was in, so he sat on his rock in the place where they'd practised getting married, and wondered just how things had gone so wrong.

She climbed the rocks to the top, skipped over the flat rocks where she'd sat with Keanu—had it been only a few days ago?

Keanu.

He'd sorted out the problem at the mine—or would eventually—and he'd spoken to her father.

But not to her.

Did he really know her so little he'd thought she wouldn't want to know?

After all the work she'd done on the figures, of course he had to know. Had to realise the responsibility—family responsibility—she felt towards it.

And didn't he even consider just how hard this might be—hearing that a chunk of her life, her heritage, had been taken from her without any discussion?

It wasn't that she wanted the blasted mine. As long as it continued to support the hospital, she couldn't have cared less what happened to it.

Somewhere deep inside she knew she was being silly, that it was just a mine. And she knew full well that without it the hospital couldn't keep going.

She made her way along the track to the house, still feeling wounded no matter how she tried to rationalise it.

Had Keanu talked to her about his idea, made her part of it right from the start, she knew she'd probably feel differently about it.

Probably even be as excited as he was about it.

She'd reached the hospital and was about to climb the hill to the house when Sam caught up with her, his face so serious she knew something was wrong.

Very wrong!

'You father phoned,' he said gently. 'Christopher has taken a turn for the worse. He'd like you home.'

Panic flooded her body. She'd always known this day would come. Known, too, that it was getting closer.

But now...

'He's sending a plane for you. You've got two hours. You father will send a car to meet the plane at Sydney airport.'

Caroline supposed she'd heard the words, but her total focus was on her brother, willing him to stay alive until she got there.

She'd been selfish, thinking only of her own unhappiness when she'd fled to the island, and now—

Shutting off *that* thought, she hurried up to the house.

Keanu left the grotto. He'd told Reuben he'd go over to Atangi to talk to the elders again—tell them he'd spoken to Max. Reuben was phoning them and they'd be waiting for him, no doubt filled with excitement and ideas about how they'd manage the mine.

He went down to the village where he kept a boat he'd bought from one of the locals almost as soon as he'd arrived back on Wildfire, half thinking he should have let Caro know where he was going, but he was already running late.

Plus, he needed to consider her reaction before he talked to her again. Out on the water he could think straight. Right now he felt there was a lot of thinking that needed straightening. Not only was the issue of the mine hanging between them but the knowledge that he had to tell Caroline that he was free, that his divorce was final worried at him too. Just how would she react to that news? Given the sour response to his plans for the mines and his ill thought-out decision to get the ball rolling without first consulting her, he imagined that trusting him with her heart was furthest from her mind right now...

He headed towards Atangi, easing the boat over the shallow part of the reef.

The little engine pushed them through the water and the tension he'd been feeling eased.

So *was* it love he felt for her?

Adult love?

Enough to build a future on? Now that he finally had a future?

It was hard to tell because he'd always loved her and even when he'd cut her out of his life rarely a day had gone by without something reminding him of her.

And now she was here, back on Wildfire where it had all begun, and he couldn't begin to work out...

What couldn't he work out?

Whether or not he loved her?

No, that part was settled, but there were so many different kinds of love.

No, he was playing with words.

He loved Caroline, and he was pretty sure that Caroline loved him. And if that was the case they could sort out the rest.

Hadn't they talked of love on the swing?

But had he *told* Caro that he loved her?

Had he actually said the words?

He tried to think but his mind went blank with shock at his own stupidity. That he, who knew Caro probably better than anyone else did, hadn't told her how he felt.

Her whole life had been filled with the uncertainty of love. Not that she spoke of it, or wallowed in self-pity. No, his Caro just got on with things. Like being left with her grandma for a start, then boarding school, and all the times her father hadn't come. Even Christopher kept his best smiles for his father.

So of course she'd be uncertain about his love, then taking the decisions about the mine away from her—that was how she'd have seen it—would have been the last straw.

He had to see her, tell her he loved her, that more importantly he was now free to love her. He'd start with that *then* sort out the mine business. He'd see the elders, go back to Wildfire.

Full of resolve, Keanu pulled into the harbour at Atangi, thinking not of the meeting but of the night ahead.

If only Keanu was here, Caroline thought as she flew over the Pacific. With him beside her she could face anything.

Was that what love was about?

Having someone to lean on, someone there to help you through the rough times as well as celebrate the good ones? She'd been stupid, reacting as she had to Keanu's suggestion about the mine co-op. She wasn't even sure why she'd reacted as she had.

And blaming Keanu...

Though if he really loved her, the way she now realised she loved him, wouldn't she be the first person to discuss it with?

Even before he knew it might actually work?

Of course not, that was a petty and stupid way to think.

She'd been unfair, but the calm way he'd announced *he'd* sorted out the mine problem, leaving her out completely, had temporarily blocked all rational thought and she'd struck out at him.

And now, heading further and further away from him, she couldn't tell him—couldn't say she was sorry and agree it was an ideal answer to the problem, even if she felt that a little bit of herself had been cut off.

In her head, the mine had been as much a part of Wildfire as the house she knew was home.

But stuff had gone from it and the house had still been home.

She'd phone Keanu as soon as she was in the car on the way to the hospital and tell him she was sorry.

Tell him she loved him.

Tell him she needed him?

Was it too soon for that?

CHAPTER TWELVE

RETURNING TO WILDFIRE, and heading straight to the house to tell Caro he loved her—this mission becoming more urgent by the moment—Keanu was disconcerted to hear she'd gone.

Because she was upset with him?

But Bessie was still explaining and he forced himself to listen.

Christopher…Sydney…charter flight…

He thanked Bessie and headed for his villa. Thankfully, he could get the regular flight out of here the next day. He sat at his computer, booking a flight from Cairns to Sydney, and arranging a hire car to be waiting at the airport.

Praying all the while—for Christopher, for Caro and for himself a little—hoping he hadn't left all he wanted to say until it was too late.

Mrs Phipps, the housekeeper, older now and somehow smaller, opened the front door of the Lockharts' Sydney house and squinted uncertainly up at him.

'Do I know you?'

'It's Keanu, Mrs Phipps. I used to come here sometimes during the holidays to play with Caroline and talk to Christopher.'

'Keanu?'

Her voice was slightly disbelieving.

'But you're much bigger now. You've grown. Of course you've grown! But welcome. You've come to be with Caroline, I suppose. They're up at the hospital—she and Dr Lockhart. Christopher's very poorly again.'

He didn't need to ask what hospital. There was an excellent private hospital just a few blocks away and the professional staff there all knew and loved Christopher, treating him with special care.

'Thank you, Mrs Phipps,' he said and turned away.

'But don't you want to leave your bag? You'll stay here surely?'

He looked down at the bag he was carrying, having decided a taxi was easier than a hire car in a city he didn't know well.

Would he stay here?

Would he be wanted?

He wished he were as certain as Mrs Phipps seemed to be.

'Best not,' he said, 'but thanks.'

And with that he headed down the ramp, out onto the street and up the road to where the hospital was built to look out over a part of Sydney's magnificent harbour.

With the money the twins' maternal grandparents had left in trust for Christopher, he would always have twenty-four-hour care, private hospitals and the best of doctors and specialists. So this hospital was a special place, and he would be getting the best possible treatment here.

But Keanu's heart quaked at the thought of Caro losing her brother. They might not have been physically close but there'd always been a special bond between them. Even as a child, if she woke with a nightmare in the night his mother would be sure to get a call the next morning to say Christopher wasn't well.

Poor Caro.

Would she let him comfort her? Take whatever support he could offer her?

Or had he hurt her too badly for that?

Once at the hospital, he asked a friendly receptionist if he could leave his bag behind her counter, then enquired about Christopher's whereabouts.

'He's in Room 22 on the second floor, but I think it might be family only. Dr Lockhart and his sister are in with him right now. He's very frail.'

The woman blinked back tears, and Keanu realised just how special Christopher was to all those who'd come in contact with him.

He tapped gently on the closed door of Room 22 then eased it open. Max was asleep in a big chair by the bed, while Caroline was sitting close to the bed, Christopher's hand clasped in hers, her head bent over it, possibly dozing as well.

He opened the door wider, and a slight squeak made her turn.

'Keanu?'

She mouthed his name, set Christopher's hand down on the bed and got up stiffly from the chair, easing out the door and closing it behind her.

'What are you doing here?' she demanded, but fairly weakly as her exhaustion clearly showed in the shadows under her eyes and the taut lines drawn in her skin.

'I hadn't said I loved you, really loved you—the now you not the past or anything else, just you,' he replied, and realised how lame it sounded when he saw the puzzled look on her face.

'I just wanted you to know. I know I don't deserve your love after the way I treated you, but somehow it seemed important to tell you anyway. We talked all around it at times, but on my way to Atangi it came to me that I'd never said the words. Not properly...

'There, I have more I need to talk to you about, much more, but that's the crux of it,' he added a little later, when the only reaction from the woman he loved had been a bewildered stare.

'Now, how bad is Christopher? You look exhausted and I've never seen your father look so grey. Why don't you take him home for a proper sleep and I'll sit with Christopher? I'll call you the moment there's any change and don't bother about that stuff I said, just go home and rest for a while.'

'You'll sit with him?'

Teardrops sparkled on her eyelashes, and it was all he could do not to kiss them away.

'Of course I will. Don't you remember when he had measles at the island that time and I'd had them so I was okay and I sat with him every day? We like each other.'

Caro reached up and kissed his cheek.

'I'll get Dad,' she said, nothing more, but somehow Keanu felt it was enough.

For now...

Max and Caro left, Max shaking Keanu's hand in welcome, and thanks and goodbye.

'We won't be long,' he promised, 'but don't hesitate to call if there's any change.'

'I won't,' Keanu promised, then he watched them walk away, Caro turning at the door to give him a puzzled look.

Keanu took his place in the chair Caro had been using and took Christopher's hand in his, holding what was little more than a bag of frail bones and skin very gently.

He massaged the skin, just rubbing it, and, remembering himself and Caro sitting with Alkiri, he began to talk, quietly but clearly.

'It's Keanu, mate. I've sent the others home to sleep. You're causing them a bit of worry at the moment. Anyway, I'm glad I've got this chance to sit with you because there's a lot I have to tell you. I love her, you see, your sister, though I'm not sure how she feels about me. For a while there, back on Wildfire, I thought she might love me back, but I've made a bit of a mess of things so it's hard to tell.'

He paused, then continued, this time gently rubbing Christopher's withered arm, spreading cream on it he'd found on the table by the bed.

'If she does love me, mate, I want to let you know that I'll never let her down. I did before because I didn't want to hurt my mum, and then again, recently, when I told her I'd married someone else. But you have to believe me, that part of my life is over, it's really over now that my divorce has finally come through. And I swear to you, Christopher, that I will never do anything to hurt her again. She's so special, your sister, that she deserves the very best, and although I know I'm not that, I'd do my darnedest to become it just for her.'

Was it his imagination or had Christopher's eyes fluttered open, just momentarily?

Keanu kept talking, moving to the other side of the bed to put cream on the hand and arm over there. He talked of the island, of how well the hospital was doing and how much his family had done for the people of M'Langi.

He talked about the day outside, cool but cloudless so the sun sent sparkly diamonds of light dancing across the waters of the harbour.

'I guess you've seen it like this before if they always put you in this room, but it's magic to me. I'd like to buy her a diamond, but then I think of her eyes and wonder about sapphires. I don't suppose you have any idea of her stone preferences? Not that she's likely to want anything from me. I kind of did something that upset her.'

And this time the eyelids definitely fluttered, and Keanu could have sworn he'd felt a tiny bit of pressure from the claw-like hand clasped in his.

'But I guess if she doesn't love me, there's not much I can do.'

Definite pressure this time. Keanu looked up at the nurse who'd remained in the room to do the regular obs and update Christopher's chart.

'Did he move his fingers?' the young man asked. 'I'm sure he did, and his eyelids fluttered as well.'

'I'd better get the family back,' the nurse said.

'They won't have had much sleep.'

The nurse was obviously torn.

'I'll give them another ten minutes and phone the house. The housekeeper will know whether to wake them.'

'Maybe suggest she wake Caroline. I'm sure Dr Lockhart has been more sleep deprived than she has.'

The nurse did his checks, agreed that all the signs were that Christopher might be improving, then left the room.

'Of course you're improving,' Keanu said. 'I'll want you around for the wedding, you know. That's if she'll have me.'

He took a deep breath and put all thoughts of love and weddings out of his mind.

'Do you remember,' he said, letting go of his hand and moving down to massage Christopher's toes now, 'how we took you swimming in the lagoon that time you were visiting? Mum put you in a life jacket and we all lay on our backs in the water and looked up at the sky through the canopy of the rainforest.'

Christopher's eyes, so like Caroline's, opened slightly and Keanu could swear he was actually looking at him.

Christopher's smile might be but a shadow, but Keanu's answer was a broad grin.

'And what about when we took you down to Sunset Beach in your wheelchair but the path was too steep and we tipped you out, and when we got you back in, we had to spend ages wiping red sand off you so your nurse and Mum wouldn't know?'

Open eyes *and* a smile!

Keanu's hand surged with joy.

'Oh, Christopher, we had such fun!'

'Didn't we?' a quiet voice said, and Keanu looked up to see Caro on the other side of the bed.

'Where did you come from? I thought the nurse was going to let you sleep for ten minutes before she rang the house.'

Caroline came into the room and sat down in the chair she'd been in earlier. She took Christopher's other hand in hers, leaned forward to kiss his cheek, then finally looked at Keanu.

'I never left,' she said. 'I went as far as the lift with Dad then thought of something.'

She hesitated, heart pounding, knowing what she wanted so much to say, but still held back by uncertainties she couldn't name.

'Thought of something?' Keanu prompted.

She nodded, saw Christopher's eyes open, looking at her, urging her on, it seemed.

'I hadn't told you I loved you either. I'd wanted to but I hadn't. I was upset about the mine business—stupid really when it's a good idea—then Dad phoned to say he'd sent the plane to bring me home and all I could think about was Christopher. Then, when I came back just now, I heard you talking to him—I stood and eavesdropped and put my finger to my lips so the nurse wouldn't betray me and now I want to tell Christopher something too.'

She lifted his hand and pressed her lips to it.

'I love this man Keanu, Christopher, and I do hope you approve because without him I don't think I could go on. He is part of me, part of my heart and soul, and always has been, and now that I understand why he broke away, well,

I love him even more, because that was done from love—love for his mother.'

She reached across the bed and took Keanu's hand in hers.

'And in case Christopher didn't tell you, I like sapphires.'

Max, alerted by the nurse, came in to a surprising tableau. His son, who'd been lingering close to death for days, was not quite alert, but definitely had his eyes open and a lopsided smile on his face, while his daughter shone with luminous radiance, sitting with her hand linked in Keanu's across the bottom of the bed.

And Keanu's face wasn't exactly doleful either.

'You two got something to tell me?' he asked.

'I'd like to marry your daughter,' Keanu said.

'But not right away, Dad,' Caroline assured him. 'There's a lot of stuff to sort out at the island and when we're married there, I want it to be the perfect, happy, heavenly place it used to be.'

'I presume you'll let me know a date,' Max said, smiling at the pair. 'Now, I'm sure you've got plenty to say to each other so leave me with my son, and go make your plans.'

* * * * *

Don't miss the next story in the fabulous
Wildfire Island Docs *miniseries:*
The Nurse Who Stole His Heart
by Alison Roberts.
Available now

MILLS & BOON®
Hardback – February 2016

ROMANCE

Leonetti's Housekeeper Bride	Lynne Graham
The Surprise De Angelis Baby	Cathy Williams
Castelli's Virgin Widow	Caitlin Crews
The Consequence He Must Claim	Dani Collins
Helios Crowns His Mistress	Michelle Smart
Illicit Night with the Greek	Susanna Carr
The Sheikh's Pregnant Prisoner	Tara Pammi
A Deal Sealed by Passion	Louise Fuller
Saved by the CEO	Barbara Wallace
Pregnant with a Royal Baby!	Susan Meier
A Deal to Mend Their Marriage	Michelle Douglas
Swept into the Rich Man's World	Katrina Cudmore
His Shock Valentine's Proposal	Amy Ruttan
Craving Her Ex-Army Doc	Amy Ruttan
The Man She Could Never Forget	Meredith Webber
The Nurse Who Stole His Heart	Alison Roberts
Her Holiday Miracle	Joanna Neil
Discovering Dr Riley	Annie Claydon
His Forever Family	Sarah M. Anderson
How to Sleep with the Boss	Janice Maynard

MILLS & BOON®
Large Print – February 2016

ROMANCE

Claimed for Makarov's Baby	Sharon Kendrick
An Heir Fit for a King	Abby Green
The Wedding Night Debt	Cathy Williams
Seducing His Enemy's Daughter	Annie West
Reunited for the Billionaire's Legacy	Jennifer Hayward
Hidden in the Sheikh's Harem	Michelle Conder
Resisting the Sicilian Playboy	Amanda Cinelli
Soldier, Hero...Husband?	Cara Colter
Falling for Mr December	Kate Hardy
The Baby Who Saved Christmas	Alison Roberts
A Proposal Worth Millions	Sophie Pembroke

HISTORICAL

Christian Seaton: Duke of Danger	Carole Mortimer
The Soldier's Rebel Lover	Marguerite Kaye
Return of Scandal's Son	Janice Preston
The Forgotten Daughter	Lauri Robinson
No Conventional Miss	Eleanor Webster

MEDICAL

Hot Doc from Her Past	Tina Beckett
Surgeons, Rivals...Lovers	Amalie Berlin
Best Friend to Perfect Bride	Jennifer Taylor
Resisting Her Rebel Doc	Joanna Neil
A Baby to Bind Them	Susanne Hampton
Doctor...to Duchess?	Annie O'Neil

MILLS & BOON®
Hardback – March 2016

ROMANCE

The Italian's Ruthless Seduction	Miranda Lee
Awakened by Her Desert Captor	Abby Green
A Forbidden Temptation	Anne Mather
A Vow to Secure His Legacy	Annie West
Carrying the King's Pride	Jennifer Hayward
Bound to the Tuscan Billionaire	Susan Stephens
Required to Wear the Tycoon's Ring	Maggie Cox
The Secret That Shocked De Santis	Natalie Anderson
The Greek's Ready-Made Wife	Jennifer Faye
Crown Prince's Chosen Bride	Kandy Shepherd
Billionaire, Boss...Bridegroom?	Kate Hardy
Married for their Miracle Baby	Soraya Lane
The Socialite's Secret	Carol Marinelli
London's Most Eligible Doctor	Annie O'Neil
Saving Maddie's Baby	Marion Lennox
A Sheikh to Capture Her Heart	Meredith Webber
Breaking All Their Rules	Sue MacKay
One Life-Changing Night	Louisa Heaton
The CEO's Unexpected Child	Andrea Laurence
Snowbound with the Boss	Maureen Child

MILLS & BOON®
Large Print – March 2016

ROMANCE

A Christmas Vow of Seduction	Maisey Yates
Brazilian's Nine Months' Notice	Susan Stephens
The Sheikh's Christmas Conquest	Sharon Kendrick
Shackled to the Sheikh	Trish Morey
Unwrapping the Castelli Secret	Caitlin Crews
A Marriage Fit for a Sinner	Maya Blake
Larenzo's Christmas Baby	Kate Hewitt
His Lost-and-Found Bride	Scarlet Wilson
Housekeeper Under the Mistletoe	Cara Colter
Gift-Wrapped in Her Wedding Dress	Kandy Shepherd
The Prince's Christmas Vow	Jennifer Faye

HISTORICAL

His Housekeeper's Christmas Wish	Louise Allen
Temptation of a Governess	Sarah Mallory
The Demure Miss Manning	Amanda McCabe
Enticing Benedict Cole	Eliza Redgold
In the King's Service	Margaret Moore

MEDICAL

Falling at the Surgeon's Feet	Lucy Ryder
One Night in New York	Amy Ruttan
Daredevil, Doctor...Husband?	Alison Roberts
The Doctor She'd Never Forget	Annie Claydon
Reunited...in Paris!	Sue MacKay
French Fling to Forever	Karin Baine

MILLS & BOON®

Why shop at millsandboon.co.uk?

Each year, thousands of romance readers find their perfect read at millsandboon.co.uk. That's because we're passionate about bringing you the very best romantic fiction. Here are some of the advantages of shopping at www.millsandboon.co.uk:

* **Get new books first**—you'll be able to buy your favourite books one month before they hit the shops

* **Get exclusive discounts**—you'll also be able to buy our specially created monthly collections, with up to 50% off the RRP

* **Find your favourite authors**—latest news, interviews and new releases for all your favourite authors and series on our website, plus ideas for what to try next

* **Join in**—once you've bought your favourite books, don't forget to register with us to rate, review and join in the discussions

Visit **www.millsandboon.co.uk**
for all this and more today!